# Ubiquitous

# Medical

### A Novel

## Dale J. Moore

Dale J. Moore

Ubiquitous Medical / Dale J. Moore - 1st Edition Trade Paperback

ISBN 978-0-98128176-6

This book and others by Northern Amusements are available in electronic format. Visit our web site at www.northernamusements.com.

e-Pub version
ISBN 978-0-98128177-3
e-PDF version
ISBN 978-0-98128178-0

Cover by Dale J. Moore
Author photo by Linda Moore
Edited by Maureen P. Moore
Printed and bound in the Canada and/or the United States.

2

# <u>Dedications</u>

**To my family, for their love, support, and inspiration.**

# Table of Contents

# *1* Home

His earliest memory entails being led away from his parents. Memories and dreams are two of a kind, separated only by the truth of reality. Sometimes they are difficult to discern and together they love to play tricks on the old, the troubled, and the lonely. Memories can be distorted by personal perception, or just the time that has vanished since they first appeared. That earliest memory shows smiles and tears, joy and sadness, and the recollection of confusion over which sentiment he should feel. But he was young at the time and this memory has been replayed so many times that the clarity and resolution are fading. At times internally incoherent, and distorted with so many unfulfilled reunion dreams, the memory is blurred to where it now baffles his otherwise brilliant mind. If his childhood reminder did not still adorn his headboard, he'd quite possibly convince himself the memory was indeed a dream.

Just as the buzz of the alarm broke the silence of the morning, so did the light of the projected clock disrupt the darkness of his bedroom. A swipe of his hand through the air penetrated the clock's image and terminated the familiar morning tone. The motion also triggered the drapes to part, filling the room with sunlight. The light did not have much to shine upon, as his king sized bed sat solitary in the room. Justin2707 was anxious to get his mind and his day going. Seven A.M., the same time he awoke every day. Every day for as long as he could remember. Lights went out at 22:00 hours, and rise and shine at 7:00 hours. Today was a day to shine.

Justin2707 moved from his barren sleeping quarters to his equally stark bathroom. Thirty seconds in the sonic shower to freshen up and he'd almost be ready for the day. He pondered what a hot water shower must have felt like. He had heard that they were refreshing, but the thought of hot water pouring all over his body seemed kind of creepy. A thick mop of brilliant red hair topped his lean six foot two inch build and he wondered how long his hair would stay wet after a water shower. It sounded awfully uncomfortable, possibly dangerous, and like a huge waste of water. Of course, fifty years ago people wasted water on all kinds of things that would be deemed silly or even irrelevant now. It still bothered him that he had to sit on a toilet and flush his waste with water. Perhaps he'd work on micro-bodies for that in his spare hours in the evening, if he could find a few sometime.

Getting dressed never posed a challenge. The small closet contained four neatly organized compartments. One for white t-shirts; one for orange scrubs; one for underwear; one for socks. Three lab coats, all white, hung beside the compartments. The laundry drop was positioned on the other side of the closet. Every two days the compartment restocked automatically.

The aroma of hot cinnamon oatmeal, with the slightest touch of honey, enticed him to the kitchen. A tall glass of orange juice sat beside it, pulp free the way he liked it. He sat down to eat at the lone chair in front of the bar.

"Correspondence," he spoke in a slightly loud, but somewhat cracking voice, having not used his vocal chords yet this morning. An image of a screen appeared in the air in front of him.

"You have three new correspondences," a woman's voice replied.

Justin2707 glanced at the quicksum line for each message, as he took the first taste of his morning oatmeal.

"Parents," he said. He listened to their message intently. When the messaged ended, he decided he wanted to play it again later that night. He didn't think he could make it through a day without getting a message from them or hearing their voices. "Recall tonight at twenty hundred hours."

He read through the quicksum line of the next, which read 'Nagesh1410 – protein analysis.'

"Nagesh1410 ... transfer to lab FID". This requested the document be made active on the Floating Interactive Display in the lab area of the adjoining work room.

He moved onto the next correspondence which read 'Chantelle0206 ... enzyme analysis.'

"Chantelle0206 ... transfer to lab FID. Please close kitchen FID."

The display evaporated into the air as quickly as it had materialized, before Justin2707 could even fully get off his bar seat. As he pushed away from it, the surface of the bar lowered into a previously undetectable cavity. The dishes were instantly gathered for cleaning and gone from view. The counter restored itself to a clean level surface. He grabbed the mouth cleansing gum that came presented with his breakfast. A few quick chews as he walked were enough to clean all the surfaces of his teeth and gums, as well as freshen his breath as it dissolved.

The bedroom, bathroom, and kitchen were small, unadorned rooms. He didn't care or even notice, but then how much room does one person need for basic functions anyway? The lab room, on the other hand, was large and well utilized. Equipment stood wedged into every available space of a room that would look cavernous if empty. He had room to comfortably move between stations, but no space for additional machines. Justin2707 believed the housing must be pretty similar for all the researchers, having paid attention to the backgrounds of the live correspondences from many of his peers as they worked.

"Recall Nagesh1410," he spoke as he neared a desk that had a few small stacks of paper on it. In spite of all the technology that he'd grown up with, and remained at his disposal, he still liked to occasionally write things down the old-fashioned way. He had endured ridicule a few times about the habit by some of his peers when they caught a glimpse of his desk on the two-way FID. With the utterance of his command, the lab FID activated about a metre in front of him and began playing the message. Nagesh1410 spoke about the results of the most recent protein analysis, as it transferred the data to Justin2707's analyzer.

"Chantelle0206," he spoke, and a similar video message and data transfer took place as the FID preceded him as he moved from the desk to the analyzer.

"Compare results to Orchid baseline. Present results in tabular format using fourteen KPI's, highlighting the KPI's that are out of acceptable variance range."

He sat down in front of the analyzer and waited patiently, but only momentarily, for the results. The display read 'All variances within acceptable range.' Details for the fourteen representative key performance indicators were presented. Twelve of the fourteen indicators showed zero occurrences, not even a slight variance. The other two indicators showed variances of less than half the acceptable margin.

"Simulate human aging and re-present results in tabular format using fourteen KPI's, highlighting KPI's out of acceptable variance range. Show results at three year aging increments; sample age is forty-five; ending age is one hundred and eight. Secondly, perform reverse aging analysis with sample starting age of forty-five and ending age of thirty."

A considerable wait lay ahead of him. He anticipated a wait of many hours for the results, so he called Chantelle0206. As team leader, he should likely wait until the final results were in from his latest simulation before sharing the findings and next steps with the whole team. But he often looked for an excuse to talk to Chantelle0206. A striking brunette, her soft looking bronzed skin stayed in his mind. He was often distracted by her luminous brown eyes that, at times, sent him into a trance. In spite of his years of dedication to medical research and lifetime of training in concentration and focusing techniques, he would find his mind wandering into those eyes and completely lose moments in time. He'd never met a woman like her before and was quite awestruck. Though in reality, he'd never met any woman.

# 2 *The Daily News*

Bruce Templeton fiddled slightly with his tie as he adjusted the microphone attached to it. The other two announcers were much less fidgety than Bruce and sat quietly reviewing their notes in front of them.

"Don't touch your tie!" hollered a petite woman off to the right of the modest soundstage. The well-dressed, partially greying, but still youthfully handsome Bruce looked up sheepishly. He acknowledged the comment by moving his hands to the desk and clasping them together. The other announcers didn't even look up, knowing thirty seconds remained to transmission time and, as usual, Bruce was the target of her threat.

The thirty seconds gave way to an up-tempo bit of music that sounded out of place for a news show. It fit perfectly though for this news show.

"Welcome to another morning of news the way we interpret it!" Bruce bellowed over the fading music, his voice resonating much too loudly by the end of the sentence.

"That's the way we tell it, Bruce. We don't hide the truth, because quite frankly, we don't really know what it is." The response came from the lone woman on the news trio, Ingrid Lindstrom, also the youngest of the group. Attractive, but not model-like gorgeous; and below average beauty for a newswoman.

"And we don't really care, because nobody else seems to," Tulio Mandovi said, the third leg of the successful news spoof. He didn't have the anchorman looks of Bruce, but his elastic facial abilities were relied upon regularly.

"Today the President spoke to the media for the first time about his alleged affair with Monique Presquile," Bruce began the first story. A still picture of the President occupied the background of the screen. "He of course denied the allegations." Bruce usually delivered the straight line of the first story, and played the role of place setter for the smarmy remarks of Ingrid and Tulio.

"All of this despite the FID footage of him kissing Miss Presquile." Ingrid fanned herself with her hand and rolled back her eyes, suggesting an erotic nature to the clip.

"When asked about this footage, the President initially claimed it was faked. When asked how someone got around his government's stringent anti-correspondence-forging security software, he retracted his claim of malicious editing." Tulio smiled at a picture showing the President looking confused with question marks bouncing around his head.

"Since the President offered no explanation, we have come to the conclusion that Miss Presquile had something lodged in her throat and the President took the most appropriate and heroic action of jamming his tongue in there to relieve the blockage," Ingrid finished.

The active camera shifted back to Bruce.

"In other news, we spotted UbiquiMed's eighty-seven year old CEO coming out of this swanky night club in Los Angeles." Arthur Antonelli's face filled in the background.

"Yes indeed, Bruce. And it appears that UbiquiMed has developed the cure to aging. As you can see here, Mrs. Antonelli appears to be only in her early twenties."

"Watch this footage as we ask Mr. Antonelli to discuss this new wonder drug."

"Sir, can we speak with you?" The video clip showed Mr. Antonelli exiting the club with his female companion, pushing his way through the line of people waiting to get inside. Bruce pressed a microphone toward Mr. Antonelli's face. "Sir, we are just wondering why you aren't taking the anti-aging pills like your wife here? She looks fantastic for a woman of seventy-five!"

Mr. Antonelli looked back at them, at first with a look of anger, then with a slight grin as he followed his companion into a waiting teleporter.

"That was an excellent question you asked him, Bruce," Tulio added.

"Yes, he gave no indication when this pill would be on the market though."

"It certainly is good to see that the billions of tax dollars pumped into UbiquiMed by our government for research are *finally* producing tangible results again."

"Yes, it has been a few years since the program's last announced breakthrough, and Mr. Antonelli's company has come under recent pressure from various government watchdogs."

"Apparently the pressure hasn't prevented Mr. & Mrs. Antonelli from enjoying themselves."

"Uh, Tulio, I don't think that was Mrs. Antonelli … " Ingrid got cut off by Bruce with precision timing.

"And that's the news as we see it for today. Remember, the story is more important than the truth. Because …" and Bruce paused for a second to allow them all to join in.

"Such is Life!"

"Cut! Great show everyone. We're already getting correspondences," the petite woman bellowed across the set as she had one eye on the stage and one on the FID in front of her.

The producer, and the advertisers, measured the success of a show by the number of correspondences received, as did the new Nielsen rating system. The switch had occurred after the media was allowed to begin transmitting again 10 years ago.

"Such is Life" had transmitted for a couple of years, with generally strong ratings. The addition of Bruce boosted ratings to new heights, as he had come off a hugely successful comedy show of his own. He had aspired to become a serious newscaster when he came out of college with a major in politics. He auditioned for every show and broadcaster at the time, but could never land a spot. Everyone wanted someone with previous experience, a detriment for someone fresh out of school.

His break came just as he feared a dead-end on the audition road. He got a call-back, but as a background reporter checking sources for stories. Bruce wasn't interested at first, but it was work. He also figured what the heck; it might lead to something else. And it did. For one, he met Roy Goodwyn. Within a few years, Bruce began writing for the show as well. While he desired screen time, the writing residuals paid off.

Then his world collapsed. All broadcasts were suspended during the Dark Years, replaced by government-controlled shows. When the broadcast blackout lifted, significant competition existed for jobs. The government still limited and monitored broadcasts, so jobs were scarce, in front of and behind the camera. Bruce landed a spot role on a comedy show that led to a full time supporting role on the same broadcast. After six years in total on that broadcast, he received an offer of his own spin-off show.

The Bruce Templeton show ran for two years, and stood as the top rated show for all but the first three episodes. He began to tire of working on a show where his writing contribution remained more or less limited to ad-libbing during recording. The show provided good experience, and admittedly great exposure, but now he wanted to get back to his original goal. Unfortunately, due to great success in a comedic role, nobody wanted to take a chance that he'd be taken seriously doing broadcast news. "Such is Life" was born partly out of frustration with the rejection, and mostly out of his desire to express his disillusionment with those who were running the country and how they were running it.

The broadcast allowed him to inject his personal viewpoint into the stories. Bruce had become increasingly bothered by today's politicians. He'd studied the history of politics before the Dark Years, and saw alarming parallels between then and now. All of the scandals were great for a show like "Such is Life", but illustrated how politicians were showing less responsibility to their public and were slowly becoming more abusive of their position and the power it brought. He just hoped that abuse of power couldn't creep into the broadcast system like it had as a precursor to the Dark Years. After all, his show made fun of these people in power, and those shows had been the first targets of repression and violence the last time.

# 3 *The Big Day*

"Deborah ... have you seen my good belt?" Peter had looked everywhere for his new black belt.

"It's in your closet, on the hanger with your suit and shirt for the interview." Deborah had done a lot of planning for this day.

Peter heard her response and looked at himself in the mirror. He had already dressed, but not in the outfit designated as appropriate by Deborah. At least this time he knew in advance of coming out of the bedroom that he needed to change. Usually he got dressed for an event only to have Deborah say something like "You're not wearing that are you?" This was a definite clue, even for him, to ask what she had planned for him to wear. Another one of his favourite sayings, "hurry up and get changed," would be spoken as he entered the room already dressed for the event in clothes he'd picked out.

"Thanks," was his simple reply.

"Just hurry! We only have forty-five minutes to get over there." Deborah knew they actually had an hour, but also knew what a dawdler Peter was. She figured if a fire broke out in their home that he'd never make it out alive. He'd get distracted by some thought in that brain of his and forget to leave the house. So while a thing like taking their baby boy to an interview should be a simple thing, she needed to keep Peter on task at every minute.

"I'm ready!" Peter proudly exclaimed, entering the living room.

"Your belt, dear."

"Oh, yeah." Peter felt his waist, then turned back to the bedroom.

Deborah held their baby boy. Dressed up in a little suit and tie, his hair stayed neatly combed back. She had applied some gel to hold it in place. Everyone said that he looked like his mother, but he was Daddy's boy. Mother provided regiment for her son, while Daddy provided love and nurturing. When it came to his boy, Peter had no problem with his attention span.

"All set," Peter announced, re-entering the living room.

"Daddy!" His son held out his arms, squirming to get free from his mother's grasp.

"Fine. Take him," and Deborah handed him to Peter. "Just don't lose him on the train."

Peter gave her a look, but only after she turned her back.

They headed out the door of their unit, with Deborah locking up behind them. The train was only a short walk away. Deborah looked at her watch and knew that there were still four trains that would allow them to get to the interview on time. She no longer worried about arriving late. Now she could worry about the interview.

Peter had spent some time prepping his son for the interview, but mostly he provided relief to Deborah's onslaught of math flash cards, physics concepts, and biology quizzes. Deborah's methods bothered Peter, and it had led to more than a few arguments in their

**18**

home. The whole concept of saturating a three year old with information bothered Peter. He understood the pressure for Deborah, and also was aware of the studies conducted in recent years that showed the massive learning potential of infants exposed to such techniques. Peter well knew the financial and social status rewards that could be theirs with acceptance of their son into the program.

Deborah had an ongoing battle with Peter about their son's training. An uphill struggle at first, Peter looked to have come around the last few months. Their boy's ability to absorb facts topped off the charts in testing she had administered. She had spent the last year monitoring and adjusting his diet and daily routine. Proud of what she had accomplished with her son, she felt certain that they would get accepted.

"Let's do some math." Deborah reached in her bag to pull out the cards.

Peter glared at her, his eyes telling her that this was not the time. Normally she'd have put Peter in his place, but Deborah didn't want to do anything to distract her son today so she let it slide.

"Just kidding, big guy. You're going to get to do some math at the nice building that we are going to. You're going to get to do all kinds of fun things."

Peter looked up the reflective glass facing of the UbiquiMed building. As the front doors sensed their arrival and opened, he heard the all too familiar slogan greet them in an unseen, yet pleasant female voice. 'Welcome to UbiquiMed. We're Everywhere, For You!'

"Mr. & Mrs. Lucas to see Mr. Reynolds," Deborah informed the receptionist upon entering the waiting room with their son.

"Thank you, Mrs. Lucas. We have all of the prerequisite forms that you sent us. If I could have the three of you go to the IDtron around the corner to my right, we'll get your fingerprints and retinal scans to confirm your identification."

Peter wasn't really crazy about having to go through these scans everywhere he went, just to prove who he was. Deborah took it as a matter of course and national security, and didn't think twice about it. Peter wasn't as trusting of the government or the medical industry. They were both getting too big and powerful for his liking. He grew concerned the government was reverting to its old ways, just before the Dark Years. Peter also worried that the government had given Ubiquitous Medical, known commonly as UbiquiMed, a monopolistic advantage when they emerged from the Dark Years. It proved a great solution at the time to hand the nation's medical care to a sole provider that had the government's financial backing. It calmed the fears of citizens, regardless of which political faction they supported. The solution provided the same calming that occurred after the banking crisis a few years earlier, which in fact had started the Dark Years. The difference being the banking industry had returned to private industry. Some privatization of the medical industry had begun, although sluggishly, no doubt by UbiquiMed's hand. That kind of power worried Peter.

"Mr. and Mrs. Lucas," a voice called from across the room. A tall dark haired man approached them as they finished with their ID scans. A doctor's lab coat obscured his suit and tie.. An UbiquiMed badge clipped to the coat's pocket showed his name in bold black letters across the top. Solomon could be seen in small print, with a larger Reynolds below it.

"Mr. Reynolds. I'm so pleased to finally meet you! I've been waiting for this day for some time." Deborah expressed her excitement with a firm grip of his hand as she shook it.

"I'm glad you're so enthused about our program. We'll take your son in for his testing, and then I'll come back out and we'll go through some information. If he's accepted, and you agree, we'll sit down and go through the rest."

"Terrific. I've got many questions."

"Let's get your boy going first, shall we?" He reached out his hand to the child, who held onto Peter's hand. The boy didn't to want to go, and his father remained equally uncertain. Peter finally gave him a pat on the behind and told him that he'd see him in a little bit.

As Mr. Reynolds and her son walked through the secured doors and down the hall beyond them, Deborah turned to her husband. Tears dropped down each of their faces. Her tears were of joy. His tears were of sadness.

Dale J. Moore

# 4 *The Cure*

Seven hours had passed since Justin2707 made his aging simulation query. The results were at last back. The next four hours were consumed reviewing every detail for every year in painstaking detail. He could find no variances that came anywhere near causing an alarm. *His team had finally done it.* Now he needed confirmation.

"Package results and distribute to Nagesh1410 and Chantelle0206. Include recorded video, beginning now…" With haste, he ran his fingers through his hair in a lame attempt to tidy it up for the video. He then began a very detailed technical description of the Orchid tests, the simulations run, and an analysis of the results. He concluded with a recommendation to proceed with trials on replica subjects.

Advances in replica subject research were remarkable in the past few years alone. The lab now had the capability to produce a whole lifetime of results from a replica in a matter of days. These replicas were not like clones. They did not experience any degeneration of materials as they aged. They could be programmed to simulate aging in an abbreviated time, so their bodies were perfect for experiments that required analysis of drug impacts over time. They also did not have any capacity to think or act for themselves. The replicas were essentially a human body devoid of any of the human qualities.

"Check correspondence reminders," he requested to his FID.

"One reminder. Have not responded to correspondence from parents."

"What time is it?"

"23:47"

"Send following note: 'Busy day, sorry I missed you. Love Justin2707.' Cancel reminder." He was too tired to send a detailed correspondence tonight. Besides, tomorrow was their scheduled live meeting day, so he'd see them then. For now he'd just grab a light snack and drink before bed.

He'd spent a little extra time on the workout machines today due to the long wait for results. He enjoyed going out to the sunroom which housed the workout equipment. He had a beautiful view of the valley and the other distant mountains. He enjoyed the fresh air during exercise.

From his treadmill he could see a few of the other units and their sunrooms. Occasionally he would catch a glimpse of another person doing their workout. He wasn't sure, but he thought he caught a glimpse of Chantelle0206 one morning. Her unit looked less than thirty metres away, but he hadn't spotted the female runner again. Personal discussion was banned from their correspondences, so he couldn't ask her. Not that he knew how to ask her. He didn't know his own address. He didn't even know if she or Nagesh1410 were even located in the same UbiquiMed complex as him. The company had numerous science lab clusters. For security purposes, he assumed they were spread all around the country.

While he worked out, he thought about all the people that the Orchid cure would help. He knew the world was tough out there, away from the shelter and luxury that the scientists lived in. Anything that he could do to make life easier for others and future generations, was definitely worth the long hours and solitude. He was anxious to get the results back and hoped to pass the live trials with flying colours. The Peach project lay next for his team, and he didn't want to keep that waiting. But he also knew the importance of focus to finding these cures. He was very confident that Orchid would lead to expediting the other cures, such as Peach.

He also let his mind wander back to Chantelle0206. He wondered if they'd ever meet. Perhaps at the announcement of the Orchid cure, they would bring his whole team together to celebrate and get recognition. But then again, with times so tough for so many, maybe a celebration could be considered a little selfish. Even a simple reception would be great. He'd truly like to look in her eyes and talk to her, not having to concentrate on the information coming out of her mouth.

Dale J. Moore

# 5 *The Results*

"Sit down please," Mr. Reynolds motioned to the Lucases to take seats around a table in his office.

"Your son is quite extraordinary! His scores are as fine as any we've seen before. You have taught him well, but most impressive are his processes of comprehension, inference, decision-making, and adaptive learning. He also showed signs beyond simple tactical planning and into strategic planning. He registered a strong capacity for both abstraction and concretization, which is exceptional in a three year old. His concentration and reasoning show great potential." Mr. Reynolds flipped through a folder that apparently held the results.

The Lucases looked at each other. They knew their boy was bright, but this praise exceeded their expectations.

"You can get all of that from the tests you run?" Peter asked, still overwhelmed by the results. "From tests you run on a three year old?"

"Yes. We have him perform certain mental drills and analyse his brain waves as he processes the information and completes the drills. It's all very non-intrusive, yet very detailed and extremely accurate in its findings." Mr. Reynolds opened the folder slightly, only to change his mind and close it. He continued speaking as he stood, stepping out from behind his desk.

"Let's just bring up the results here on the screen." He touched a few icons on the screen, causing the charts to appear..

"It sounds incredible. And these are our boy's charts?"

"Yes. See here ..." as he pointed to a line on the screen. "The black line near the middle represents the mean result for this particular test. The yellow line above that represents the 84th percentile. The higher blue line represents the 97.5th percentile. The green diamond represents your son's score. It is beyond the 99.8th percentile represented by the red line, and higher than any prior score. This test result is particularly impressive, but all of his test results put him in the upper five percentile. He set new top score in five categories. Out of seventeen that's quite impressive."

"So he's a genius?" Deborah questioned.

"We do not like that term around here. Too many negative connotations based on mental breakdowns of past so-called geniuses. We prefer the term Bright Light."

Peter wanted to find out more details than the brief few afforded in the advance materials or in their discussion earlier that day while they tested his son.

"Can you tell us more about the program?"

"Certainly. We call it Future Focus, as you know from the advance materials."

"Yes, I've seen the advertisements as well."

"Good. It's nice to see our advertising dollars are working. Anyway, we've had many studies over the past twenty years, starting before the Dark Years actually, on how the brain evolves. Those studies focused on not only the scientific and physiological aspects of development, but on the human interaction aspects. Industry research has shown that the human brain's greatest potential for learning is between ages three and nine. We performed independent studies. Using and modifying our techniques based on the documented results, we've expanded that window up to age fifteen. In fact, we've almost doubled that peak learning window in the last ten years. And furthermore, we've reduced the drop-off after that window to a more gradual rate."

"So what's the catch?" Peter asked, receiving a very stern look from Deborah in the process.

"The catch, as you call it, is that the students have very focused studies. They learn year round, not just eight or nine months of the year like many conventional schools. We also break their learning into multiple discreet sessions during the day, the number and duration of which change with the student's age. The attention span improves as they learn focus, but the brain still has limitations that can't be ignored."

"It sounds so precise and organized." Deborah by nature found these traits very appealing.

"So how long is their day? It sounds like we'll be dropping him off early and picking him up late." Peter fidgeted a bit in his chair as he posed the question.

"You don't. The children stay here with us."

"What?!!" Peter now sat up straight. Deborah squirmed in her chair, avoiding eye contact with her husband.

Mr. Reynolds looked over at Deborah, somewhat surprised and upset. She continued to hold her head down in embarrassment.

"You didn't tell him, did you?" Mr. Reynolds asked her. "I know it sounds horrible, but I don't make the rules. I sympathize with your concern," he tried to reassure them. "They believe it minimizes distraction."

Peter was getting more agitated the more he thought about it.

"Look at me, Deborah." Peter waited until she reluctantly lifted her eyes. "You knew? How could you not mention something like this?"

"We can see him anytime we want. That's part of the arrangement, right Mr. Reynolds?" Deborah tried to bail herself out. This program meant more to her than her own career, which was *really* saying something. She wanted the best education possible for her son. The status of having a child in the program meant something in the circles she lived in. And even if the parents weren't allowed to discuss the details with anyone, per the contract terms, it was well known whose children were in it. She knew executives in her firm who were promoted on their child's acceptance alone.

"Yes, Mrs. Lucas. You can see your boy any time, before, after, or between sessions. We just want a few hours' notice to schedule it properly."

"And there is a one month trial period too." Deborah continued to plead her case.

"It's a three month trial period now. We found parents were still too emotional after only one month. Three months brings about more rational decisions."

"I can definitely see why they'd be emotional. And what does all of this cost us?" Peter tried to throw another wet cloth on the idea.

"Nothing. Actually, we pay you." Mr. Reynolds sat back in his high back chair as he said it, knowing this was often the winning point in the match.

"You what?"

"We pay you, Mr. Lucas."

"Why would you pay us?"

"For one, we gain invaluable research data by studying and measuring your child as he learns. For two, we do retain patent and licence rights over anything developed by the children up to age twenty-five."

Peter saw their angle. "Those rights could add up to a lot of money."

"Twenty two years of the finest teachers available can add up to a lot of money, not that you could find teachers of the same quality at any private school. Accommodations, food, and clothing for twenty two years can also add up. Besides, we retain rights, but there is a nominal percentage payable to either the child or parents, depending upon age when the patent is approved. A small percentage can add up to huge sums of money in our industry."

Deborah looked over at Peter, pleading without saying a word.

"Fine. We'll try it for the three months and see how it goes."

"Wonderful. I'll get the agreements in here for signatures. Your son's future just got brighter."

"Like a Bright Light!" Deborah exclaimed.

Dale J. Moore

# 6 *An Old Friend*

Turning the street corner on foot, Bruce looked up to see the office tower that held the television studio for 'Such is Life.' His almond vanilla coffee was welcome warmth on a cool morning, and his eyes instinctively closed as he savoured the fresh brew. Traffic cleared, and he crossed the street with the flow of the crowd, not completely aware of his surroundings as he still relished the first taste of his coffee. If aware, he would have heard his name when it was called the first time, not on the fifth call.

"Bruce," came the shout from close behind.

Bruce finished walking across the street before turning to see who'd called his name.

"Roy? What brings you downtown?"

"I left the serenity of my home, and the bliss of retirement just to see you, believe it or not."

"I didn't think anything could drag you back down here."

"So you know it's important. Can we go somewhere to talk?"

"Sure. How about the studio? I'm sure a lot of people would be thrilled to see you again. Or at least try to collect old debts from you."

"I'm sure. But it's private." Roy looked nervously around, prompting Bruce to do the same, not knowing what he was looking for.

"We can just sneak into my office. Nobody will know you're there."

"No! We can't go into the studio. I'd have to sign in, and someone would spot me."

"Okay. Okay. I get it. Privacy…" Bruce scanned their surroundings, then grabbed Roy by the arm for a second. He let go, and without saying anything, Roy knew to follow him. Bruce led him toward the adjacent alley. Glancing around for onlookers, and not spotting anyone, Bruce put his hand on Roy's back and they ducked into the sunless alley. Ten metres down the empty alley, they stopped.

"Alright. You have my attention. What's so cloak and dagger?"

"Bruce, you've known me a long time now, so consider the source when I tell you this."

Roy was right. They had known each other many years. Roy was the producer who got Bruce the reporting job right out of school, and the one who called him for that comedy show after the Dark Years. If not for Roy, Bruce might be doing news research in a cluttered archive room somewhere, digging through mountains of paper from before the Dark Years, while his sanity slipped away. While Roy had the career that Bruce wanted, jealousy never entered the picture. Bruce learned a great deal from Roy, who mentored him on many aspects of making a living in broadcasts, news or otherwise.

"You're the best news source I've ever known," Bruce told him.

"So listen to me when I tell you to stay away from the UbiquiMed stories. Mr. Antonelli is not happy. What I'm saying is that if you don't stop on your own, they will stop you." Roy kept looking left and right to both ends of the alley, on guard for anyone watching them.

"What do you mean they'll stop me? Will they pressure the network to cancel my show?"

"I doubt it. UbiquiMed doesn't dance around their problems. They eliminate them. I'm sure you know what I mean now." Roy nervously rocked back and forth as he spoke.

"You can't just put yourself out there like that, broadcasting stories about UbiquiMed and Antonelli. Sure, I used to put myself out there, but we ensured we had a substantial following first. It took years of back- room meetings to get enough people in the right positions of authority to make a difference. One guy on a news spoof show won't even be missed, let alone treated as a martyr for the cause of bringing down UbiquiMed." Roy's face showed his anxiety, and he started walking away. Bruce once again grabbed his arm, this time looking him square in the eyes.

"I wasn't out to bring down UbiquiMed. They are just a wonderful source for stories. Everyone knows this stuff is going on. It's on the regular news for crying out loud. All we do is magnify it a bit and make it funny instead of gossipy."

"We all know his marriage is a farce and that he cheats with any young thing that will tolerate him. That's not the issue. The problem is that you've made mention many times over the past few weeks about how UbiquiMed hasn't come up with any new cures recently. The government gives them billions of tax payer dollars every year for some of their research programs. They don't want anybody highlighting their recent track record or possibly bringing the value of the investment to question."

Roy pulled his arm back slightly and Bruce let go of his grip.

"Sorry, Roy ..." Bruce uttered as he let go. "I feared that I observed some of the warning signs, but didn't think it had progressed this far yet. Doesn't this bother you, Roy? Isn't this what happened at the start of the Dark Years? Suppression of truth? Fear of the power of the government? Are you too old and too tired to fight, Roy?"

"Yes, I am. Besides, it's not my fight anymore. And I don't think it should be your fight right now either." Roy started to walk away, then stopped, turned, and made one last comment.

"Remember what I taught you, Bruce. Fame is fleeting. Don't make your life the same."

# 7 *The Early Days*

Roy Goodwyn had been a rising media star when he first had occasion to meet Bruce Templeton. Roy had used his status to freely interrupt the head recruiter during an interview. Opening the door to the office, the sight of the twenty-something daughter of the West Coast Managing Director surprised Roy. At a few parties over the years, Roy had become acquainted with her. An extremely pretty young girl, her interests lay in fashion, not broadcasting, from what he recalled.

"Sorry, Larry. Hello, Annie, good to see you again. What brings you here?"

"I'm interviewing for the on-scene reporter job. Daddy says I'll get to see all kinds of cool things, meet famous people, and get my own wardrobe," her smile lit up the room as she finished.

She had the looks to work in front of the camera, that wasn't in doubt. And she wasn't stupid, but would certainly have to lose that bubbly college girl routine to be taken seriously. But then again, she was probably going through a phase. Or perhaps 'Daddy' wanted her out earning a paycheque to see how the real world worked. Whatever the case, the job belonged to her, even if a re-incarnated Walter Cronkite walked through the door.

The head recruiter broke Roy's thoughts. "What did you want, Roy?"

"Oh, yes. I wanted to confirm that you've approved my vacation next month."

"Yes, I have. Now if you'll excuse us …"

"Certainly. It was nice to see you again, Annie," and he shook her hand.

"You too, Mr. Goodwyn. Maybe we'll get to do a story together!"

Roy feigned a smiled at the thought, closing the door on his way out. Exiting the recruiting area, he noticed the well-dressed young man in the waiting area. Something about the man grabbed Roy's attention. The recruit looked confident and his face looked instantly trustworthy. Feeling pity, or perhaps wanting to stir the pot, Roy sat down and introduced himself.

"Roy Goodwyn," and he extended his hand.

"Yes, sir. I know who you are. I'm a fan of your work. Pleasure to meet you," the young man responded as they shook hands.

"And you are?"

"Bruce Templeton, sir."

"I appreciate your manners, Bruce, but you're making me feel old with all the 'sir' stuff."

"Sorry, Mr. Goodwyn."

"So you're here for the on-scene reporter job, I assume?"

"Yes. I'm well qualified, but quite frustrated so far with interviewing."

"It is a tough industry to break into; was even in my day."

"Any advice for my interview?"

Roy held off telling him the interview was a lost cause. "Just tell me why you want this job."

"I don't want *this* job. I want your job."

Cocky bastard, Roy thought. *I like him already.* Roy let the young man continue.

"But I know there is a lot to learn. I'm sure you paid some dues to get where you are now."

"If you call jobs in ten markets the size of postage stamps putting in your dues, then I guess I did," and Roy laughed at his memories.

Interested to hear more, Bruce leaned forward and asked, "So what was your first media job?"

"Believe it or not, I went through about twenty interviews before landing a job."

"Really? And what was it, something small potatoes like I'm interviewing for today? Thirty seconds of air time, once or twice a week if lucky?"

"If you're lucky. No, worse than that I'm afraid. I was the administrative assistant to the man whose boss reported to the woman who reported to the producer's assistant."

"Wow." Bruce fell back against the back of the comfy waiting room chair, head flying back as he looked up at the ceiling. Laughing as he straightened, he said, "Was there any lower job?"

"As a matter of fact, my classmate at college wasn't as fortunate. He lacked patience, and after five interviews, took the first job that opened up here. Mail room clerk."

"Anyone I know?"

"Sadly, no. Three years in the mail room and he jumped into security, thinking it might get him closer. Three more years and the light had gone from his eyes. His dream was dead." Roy rubbed his hands together, not realizing he did so. The memory still haunted him ten years later. "There was an attempt on our producer's life, and my friend took a bullet."

"I'm sorry, Roy."

"He survived, but he was never the same." Roy's eyes looked empty, staring lost into space. "He disappeared. I heard he was living in a log cabin in the hills of Kentucky. I haven't seen him since."

Silence ensued as Roy remained in the trance of the memory. Snapping out of it, he said, "Sorry, I was lost in thought there for a minute. The moral of the story, Bruce, is don't settle, and don't give up on the dream."

"No, sir."

"And stop calling me sir!"

The head recruiter's administrative assistant came around the corner. "Sir …"

Roy and Bruce both laughed. She looked at them, briefly insulted.

"Sorry, miss, it's not you," explained Bruce.

She nodded, "He's ready for you now."

As they stood up, the daughter of the West Coast Managing Director came around the same corner.

"Annie, this is Bruce Templeton. Some day you two may be working together."

Bruce shook her hand. "Nice to meet you, Annie. What do you do here?" He immediately noticed how cute she looked, and how well dressed.

"Nothing yet, but I just interviewed for the on-scene reporter job. Keep your fingers crossed for me!"

"Okay," and Bruce crossed his fingers.

She skipped away, excited as could be.

Roy smiled at Bruce, and motioned toward the interview room.

After a polite introduction to the head recruiter, they all sat. Sitting behind a large mahogany desk, the head recruiter opened a folder holding Bruce's resume. Bruce sat up straight in the chair opposite the desk, looking very anchor-like. Roy flopped in the middle of a leather loveseat along the wall, his arms extended across the back. Roy spoke first.

"So Bruce, remember that young lady you met outside? Her name is Annie Jenkins."

"As in William Jenkins, West Coast Producer?" Bruce asked.

"Technically, his title is Managing Director. The producers report to him."

"I see ..." Bruce smiled, acknowledging Roy knew all along. He continued with tongue firmly planted in cheek, "well, I for one am glad that nepotism has no place in the media."

Roy blurted out a brief laugh, before reining it in. The head recruiter gave Roy a stern look.

The interview went on without any further interruptions or smart remarks. Roy watched how the young man handled himself. Extremely well spoken and confident, Bruce said all the right things.

Composed, he even came off as relaxed at times. Perhaps knowing he wasn't getting the job made the interview easier, Roy speculated. Whatever it was, the interviewee impressed Roy. Bruce possessed fire and passion in his eyes when he spoke, and grace caressed his voice. No nervous squeaks, twitches, or fidgeting. Roy knew this kid had a future in the media – but not this job. Roy understood the boundaries, and this job lay outside of them for Bruce.

A few weeks after the interview, Bruce got a call back. Surprised, he showed up in the same suit, to the same office. This time though, he met only with the head recruiter.

"Roy Goodwyn has continued to pester me day and night to get you a job here," the worn-down looking man told Bruce.

"Really?"

"Yes, really. The man is persistent. The job you interviewed for is taken."

"I assumed."

"We have a job, but it is not in front of the camera."

Bruce expected as much. He listened as the man continued.

"The position is for a fact verifier. You research facts in stories to make sure they are facts and not lies. It's not glamorous, but it's a start in the business. I'm not sure what this means, but Roy said to tell you that at least you shouldn't end up in a cabin in Kentucky."

Bruce smiled. "When do I start?"

# *8* *First Day of School*

In spite of Mr. Reynolds's desire to keep Peter's son after the interview and immediately immerse him in the program, the Lucases brought their son home for one last night. Their son hadn't ever slept in their bed. He did this night. Peter lay awake all night just looking at his boy, wondering if he had done the right thing. He kicked the pros and cons around his head as he lay there. His mind raced all night. Something good, something bad, something wonderful, something sad. The thoughts fought each other for Peter's attention. Surely this was what insanity felt like. Uncontrollably, his emotions bounced around the entire spectrum. How could he let Deborah talk him into this? The best education that money could buy – and free! What would he do with his time after work, the time that he usually spent with his son until bedtime. He wondered if he'd be allowed to read him bedtime stories and tuck him in at night. Peter pondered what wondrous cures his son would develop. If his son was indeed that smart, something special definitely lay before him with that kind of education.

Deborah slept for the first time in three months. She had worried about the interview and testing for six months. The last three months were agonizingly long, yet at times too short. She couldn't wait for the testing because she always felt something exceptional whenever she worked with her son. She thought at first it was just typical motherly pride, but the feelings grew more intense as she taught him. Time felt short. She had so much she wanted to teach him or get him to memorize before the test, and there simply wasn't enough time. She did have a high-paced career as well, and that made finding time for teaching a challenge. Thank goodness Peter had a more structured day than her and could provide routine to their boy's schedule. On this evening, her mind had finally stopped racing. The personal recognition she would get from this success made the sacrifice worth it. Deborah found tranquility in the test results. She slept with a smile on her face and with pleasant dreams of her son's future.

Deborah spent the morning packing a small suitcase. She put in the essentials: some basic clothing items, his toothbrush, toothpaste, comb, slippers, and a nightgown. Peter spent the morning playing with his son, making the most of their time together. With Deborah's packing complete, Peter went into his son's room to grab some personal items, slipping them into the suitcase without Deborah noticing. Peter packed a couple of their favourite Dr. Seuss books, a small picture of the three of them together, and the stuffed animal that his son slept with every night (it had also slept in their bed the night before).

At precisely 10:00 hours, the Lucas family arrived at the UbiquiMed education facility. They once again went through the process of the IDtron to confirm their identities. After passing the machine's test, they passed through a security door into a small waiting room. Solomon Reynolds entered through another security door at the opposite end of the room.

"Welcome, Deborah and Peter! I appreciate your punctuality," as he tapped his watch. "Let's get this young man started, shall we?"

"I packed him a bag with some of his things." Deborah extended the suitcase towards Mr. Reynolds.

"Oh, that won't be necessary. We have all the essentials here. And if you recall, our agreement calls for us to provide all clothing. We have uniforms for the children as we find it is one less distraction. But if you have a couple of personal items, that would be okay."

"But I didn't …" Deborah began to speak.

"There are a couple of items in there." Peter reached for the suitcase. He lay it down, unzipped it, and pulled out the books, the picture, and the stuffed animal. While still on his knees, he reached up and handed the items to Mr. Reynolds, except the stuffed animal, which he gave to his son. Peter followed with a long embrace, and a kiss that he left on his son's forehead long enough for tears to trickle off his cheek and onto the boy's face. Peter gently brushed the drops away with his thumb.

A woman dressed in a doctor's smock came through the door where Mr. Reynolds had entered. Mr. Reynolds nodded to her. She held the boy's hand, guiding him through the doors.

"Excellent. Well then, please contact our administrative staff to set up time to see your son. I suggest you give him a day or two to settle in before arranging it though. Besides, it will give us time to set up the video link."

"What do you mean, the video link?" Peter asked, re-zipping the suitcase to take it home.

"For your visits, of course."

"Thanks, but we'll just come down here."

"I'm sorry, but that won't be possible. We strive for isolation from outside distraction, and parents can be one of the most disruptive. That's why we set up the personal video link. You'll be able to watch him in his room, as well as many of the study areas anytime you like. And you'll be able to talk to him directly at pre-scheduled times."

"But our agreement allows visits…" Deborah piped in.

"The agreement states that you can 'see' your son anytime that you like. We provide a video feed to enable that. You will see that he is in excellent care and learning at an exceptional pace. Besides, this will give you more time with your baby girl."

"We only have one child…" Deborah shot a puzzled looked at Peter, then back at Mr. Reynolds.

"I told you that our equipment is very advanced here. Your retinal scans revealed that you have just become pregnant in the past few weeks."

# 9 *Solomon Reynolds*

Solomon Reynolds was a bastard. A real, honest to goodness bastard, in
multiple senses of the word. His father had had an affair for years with
Solomon's mother, the family maid, whom his father loved more than
his wife. But social standing remained important in his father's world,
so a divorce or any controversy were strictly out of the question. So
with Solomon's surprising conception and subsequent arrival, he'd
become the illegitimate child of a wealthy industrialist father and the
family maid.

Solomon was raised by his mother, who wisely saved the
regular cheques from his father. Considering the influences of the poor,
drug ravaged, and crime ridden area they lived in, it took no small feat.
The money paid for a superb education. In spite of his humble roots and
an education that most in his neighborhood would kill for, he was a
very bitter young man. Solomon could not reconcile whether the
cheques were out of love or guilt; perhaps some ill-conceived notion of
his father's about 'doing the right thing.' It tortured Solomon's teenage
soul.

Exams in his second year of university brought more weight to
his overburdened shoulders. As the economy eroded throughout the

country, it hit particularly hard in downtrodden neighbourhoods like the one he grew up in. The one his mother died in at age forty.

Word got around that Solomon had moved away to a prestigious school. A local gang figured this meant his mother had money. With banks in trouble, many people took to keeping their money at home. With Solomon gone, the taking would be easy. What the gang didn't know was that Solomon had all the money, at his mother's urging. When the gang raided his mother's house and couldn't find any cash, they tortured her, convinced she had the money well hidden somewhere in the house. The local police estimated she lay beaten and dying for almost three days before succumbing.

Solomon couldn't summon the courage to return for her funeral, never wanting to see the neighbourhood again. For years, he pictured her buried without a service or anyone there to shed a tear. Ten years passed before Solomon discovered his father had delivered the eulogy at her funeral. By then it was too late; his father had passed on as well.

That bitterness led to a fierce competitiveness and a mean streak that served him well in terms of advancing through school and his career. Second in standing in his class in his final year of medical school, the sole student ahead of him mysteriously came down with mononucleosis for six months and couldn't finish the year. Solomon finished at the top of his class. He dared his classmates to prove that he'd had anything to do with the timely demise of his competitor, confident of his virtually untraceable larceny. Solomon had injected his rival with a homemade virus after drugging the young man's drink at a class party. Preferring people knew that he meant business, Reynolds didn't even bother inflicting others to cover his trail.

His career at UbiquiMed immediately succeeded his hospital internship. Solomon could not stand working in a hospital. He didn't waste his time attempting bedside manner, feeling it beneath him to act nice to patients that needed him much more than he needed them. It wasn't that he didn't like talking with people; he just hated polite conversation. He enjoyed debating very much. He loved out-jousting other people intellectually and making them feel stupid. Nothing pleased him more than to send one of his colleagues running and crying from a room. Or running and screaming. Or wanting to punch his face. As long as he got under their skin, he had accomplished his goal. He didn't require a formal situation to humiliate someone. He preferred an audience, but did not consider it a prerequisite.

This ruthlessness served him well in moving up the corporate ladder of UbiquiMed. Those that he didn't push out of the way went running and screaming out of the way. In five years he moved up from just another insignificant research position to take over as the head of the Child Mental Assessment division. The former head of the department died in an apparent suicide. Strangely though, a body was never found, just a note. The note was neatly typed and printed on standard company letterhead.

Many at UbiquiMed thought it odd that Solomon took over this particular department. All impressions were that he didn't like kids. Truth was, he didn't like most kids because of the way most kids were reared. What Solomon did like and admire was intellect. Leading this division allowed him to devise parameters to evaluate early brain development, and more importantly, a mechanism to accurately reflect the learning potential of a brain. Five years leading this division led him to rolling out the Child Advanced Learning Method, or CALM. He felt the acronym would convince parents that everything would be fine. And selling the idea to parents was definitely required for him to get kids into the program. Solomon became very good at selling once he changed his perspective. He turned it into a challenge to intellectually paint the parents into a corner where the only logical conclusion was for them to join. If the intellectual approach wasn't working – there were artsy types he had to deal with on occasion – he could put his cold heart on hold for a short time to sweet-talk the parents until he got them to sign up their child. And he always got the ones that he wanted to sign. He could stoop to feigned emotional pleading if it meant adding a star to his program.

He liked the kids in the CALM program. Many had the potential to become as bright, or brighter, than he was. He did not have to deal with stupidity when he dealt with them – lack of knowledge perhaps – but not stupidity. One thing that he could not tolerate was stupidity.

Parents were another thing. Many of them were very smart, as you would expect from the parents of exceptional children. The first few years that he ran the program, the children were allowed daily visits with their families. Solomon got very agitated by the visits. He thought they wasted a couple of hours a day that could have been otherwise spent learning. The visits also caused other issues. Boiled down, insubordination became the problem. The parents would get the kids emotionally charged, or worse yet, plant ideas in their children's heads about how they should act and how they should be treated.

Solomon felt strongly, supported by data points, that if he could get rid of the family visits that he would increase learning by twenty-seven to thirty-six percent per year. Since part of the program funding came from the parents in the first few years, it was a tough line to cross. But determined to cross it, the obstacles didn't stand for long. With his continued recognition and advancement within UbiquiMed, Solomon got his audience with the owner, Mr. Antonelli. It took Solomon a mere twenty minutes to convince the owner to allow a pilot of the revamped program.

A small class of five kids served as the pilot. Three that scored in the middle of the pack on his assessment, plus one student each near the top and bottom were selected. He didn't want his trial tainted by studying just the best students. His initial plan to cut all parent meetings changed to allow one visit per week, a compromise with Mr. Antonelli. With the reduced interaction with parents, the children's progress improved by an average of twenty-one percent over the benchmark of previous classes. The increase held consistently with all five students. Solomon was convinced he would have reached his predicted improvement if the visits were all eliminated.

The results impressed Mr. Antonelli, so the following year Reynolds got approval to expand the approach to all classes. All classes except one, which became the pilot for the 'no visits' benchmark evaluation. Solomon did face a problem at the beginning of the year when word started to spread amongst parents that all the classes were going to this new format. He obviously would not tolerate whining parents. He also feared declining enrolment if the visitation rules were common knowledge before getting the parents hooked, or prior to selling the parents on the approach and benefits of his program. Solomon knew that he needed leverage with the parents, so his proposal to Mr. Antonelli included elimination of all fees, aside from a non-refundable application fee. The application fee was significant enough to attract only the serious, and significant enough for most people not to want to waste it by withdrawing their child.

To prevent any negative messages about the program from spreading further, he forced all the parents of current students to sign a non-disclosure agreement and threatened them with complete loss of their visitation rights if they failed to sign and uphold the agreement. New applicants were required to sign a similar agreement.

The parents of a third-year child threatened legal action, including going to the police with kidnapping charges. The parents made some initial inquiries with lawyers. Solomon knew the parents stood no chance with any legal action and that police would laugh them out of the building due to the consent forms signed during registration. Not leaving anything to chance, these parents began to receive 'anonymous' death threats shortly after the visit with their lawyer. The threats extended to their children's safety. They all signed the agreement.

# *10* *The Past and Present*

Morning came quickly this day for Justin2707. He proceeded through his normal routine of sonic shower and breakfast. This morning though, when he went to the lab, he initiated a set of tests that he had already done, logging in his journal that he wanted to reconfirm the results. He really wanted to buy time to do something on his own. He'd worked late hours the past few nights, and wanted a little bit of leisure time before his meeting with his parents.

He enjoyed history in particular. It both fascinated and disturbed him at times. Justin2707 enjoyed studying the events that led to the rapid decline of social order and the economy. He hoped to somehow make sense of it. He was conflicted that the world contained such chaos, yet he lived in a peaceful, tranquil, sheltered environment.

The articles that he could find formed a curious puzzle that he somehow felt was missing some key pieces. The timeline that he pieced together went this way: in 2061, China's economy collapsed. The lingering low pay for most labourers and government suppression became a rallying cry for the masses to overthrow the communist regime and form a democracy. The United States, of course, was heavily involved in many of the activities, although none of it officially.

The new Chinese democratic government lifted birth control rates, triggering an exponential increase in their population. The country had developed a burdensome class structure that worked fine in the old economy, but which staggered and collapsed under the weight and ideals of the new population.

In early 2062, the United States economy followed suit. The government didn't take into account the massive investment that companies from their own country had in the burgeoning Chinese economy. The ripple created crashed the U.S. economy. Canada and Mexico crashed simultaneously, their infrastructure so heavily dependent on the U.S. for exports. Europe and the rest of the world followed suit a few months later.

By late 2063, rioting and looting replaced going to work as the daily occupation of many people. There were no jobs. There was no money. There was no hope. There was only violence as people tried to survive. Martial law was declared and had remained in effect ever since - almost twenty years now.

In 2064, UbiquiMed received an exclusive contract with the U.S. government to provide universal health care for all of its citizens, a means to provide hope and security for the millions of unemployed people and their young families. Healthcare was no longer affordable under the old, almost bankrupt system. Many diseases had spread rapidly in the previous years, with cancers and other terminal illnesses on an algorithmic rise.

Prior to all of this chaos, in 2055, UbiquiMed had begun its program to train scientists. They were moved to these secure facilities in the mid 2060's, away from the distractions of the tumultuous outside world. While the program was promoted massively in the media, the program locations escaped mention. This was the program that Justin2707 entered in 2060.

What concerned him the most was the lack of articles on anything from 2065 to now, 2082. All he could find were articles related to UbiquiMed, mostly stories about their medical discoveries and how they'd 'saved the world' by implementing universal health care. He couldn't find information about *anything* during those years. He was unable to find any articles past 2062 which contained references to sporting events or cultural activities. Things were still violent and bleak out in the real world, but he found it hard to believe that all of those things came to a complete stop and never resumed. How could he not become suspicious that UbiquiMed was concealing information from him and the other scientists? After all, that was the specialty of the program – isolation from outside distraction.

Justin2707 felt confident that information existed on other computer systems outside of UbiquiMed that would provide him a more accurate view of what had gone on for the past twenty-five years, and what was happening today. It would have to wait though, as today he had a visit with his parents.

He left his lab, slipped out of his lab coat, and sat down in front of the kitchen FID. He ran his fingers through his hair, again in a lame attempt to tidy up. After thirty seconds, a voice summoned a response.

"Parents calling - live video discussion request. Accept or Decline?"

"Accept"

After a slight hesitation, his parents appeared on his FID. They were smiling, and as always, happy to see him.

"How are you doing, son?" his mother asked.

"I'm doing great. Our research is going great. We're on the verge of a major medical announcement."

"That's great, son!" his father enthusiastically replied.

"How are you two doing? Avoiding the riots okay?" At that moment the screen wavered with static lines distorting the view.

His parents leaned forward, like they didn't hear the complete message. Frustrated by the constant problems these messages experienced, Justin2707 tried to stay realistic in his expectations. After all, the world still suffered from a lot of instability beyond his secure walls. Things like power outages and communication issues were likely commonplace.

"We're doing fine." Both parents replied at the same time.

"We've got a nice trip ..." and then the transmission went awry again as his father spoke. The image returned to show his parents' hands were intertwined on the table and they were smiling from ear to ear.

"I'm sorry, I didn't get all of that. You have a nice trip, where?"

"To the ..." and static interrupted the line once again.

"Oh that's great," Justin2707 replied, not wanting to hurt their feelings that he couldn't hear them.

"We'll we're told that our time is up, son. We'll talk to you next week. Only a few more months now. Love you. Good luck with that announcement!"

"Only a few more months? What …" The image of his parents disappeared.

"Save for later replay," he told the FID.

"Turn off kitchen FID." He knew that he wouldn't be able to reconnect to his parents to find out what they meant by 'Only a few more months now.' He wasn't convinced the static resulted from trouble on the outside. It occurred consistently when something important was said. And it always truncated the message in such a way that he couldn't get enough to piece anything together. It sounded like it was edited with precision rather than a bad connection or interference. It stoked the fire of suspicion simmering in his mind. Things weren't what they seemed, and he was going to find out why they were concealing selective information from him.

Dale J. Moore

# 11 *Play Time*

Almost four years had passed since the Lucas' son entered into the UbiquiMed program. Their daughter approached her third birthday, and was every bit as bright as their son at the same age. Deborah was not fanatical about drilling her daughter with flashcards as she had with her son. Deborah played recordings of famous books, physics, or mathematical theory to her child as she slept, but not every night. She still spent considerable time teaching her child, but her methods had softened to the point where Peter accepted them.

Deborah and Peter had already decided that they were not putting their daughter into the program. They had seen their son grow rapidly in an academic sense since joining the program, yet they both missed him dearly. The three minute video calls hardly seemed like enough. Though Deborah had shown great determination to get her son into the program, she often had to reconcile in her head that she had done the right thing.

Deborah gained significant stature in her company by having a son in the program. She received three promotions, while Peter received two. Both made great strides in power and pay in their respective companies. The monthly stipend from UbiquiMed was initially a boon to the young couple, especially with a second child on the way. Now, the monthly money was gravy, dumped religiously into their daughter's education fund.

Solomon Reynolds at UbiquiMed had contacted them numerous times in the past couple of months about setting up a test time for their daughter. UbiquiMed was anxious to see how her scores compared to her brother's. The Lucases declined each request. Mr. Reynolds offered them extra video call time with their son as a bribe. As a counter offer last week, they had requested in-person visitations each week with their son, and with their daughter if she was to join. Mr. Reynolds reiterated the UbiquiMed policy about personal visits and how they were a proven distraction to the students, hindering their learning. He said that he would confer with his boss and plead special circumstances to try and get them an exception. Reynolds told them he felt their pain and would do everything he could. They did not hear back on their offer. The calls requesting a testing time stopped as well.

Deborah and Peter dressed their girl for their ritualistic Sunday walk in the park. They enjoyed getting outside to watch her play on the jungle gym, slides, and swings. It was their weekly escape from the hectic work week.

"What's it like outside today, Peter? Just wondering whether we need jackets or not."

"Gorgeous. Low twenties, with a light breeze. Low seventies as your father would say."

Their daughter wore a pretty white frilly top, light blue skirt, and white pantyhose. She looked cute as a button, as the old saying went.

"Is the wagon ready?"

"All set, how about you two?"

"All set. C'mon, dear." Deborah reached her hand out to her daughter who grabbed it. They walked out to the wagon that Peter had waiting on the front walk.

Peter locked the door behind them and walked to the front of the wagon. Their daughter sat in the little wagon with the picnic lunch as they began to wheel her to the park. The same wagon would be very useful at the end of the trip, as she almost always would be too tired to walk home, usually falling asleep curled up in the wagon with her stuffed animal.

The Lucases were so lost in their perfect Sunday walk to the park that they didn't notice they were followed. Not that they should have noticed. The people following them were paid to render themselves invisible and were very good at what they did.

The family stopped at the entrance to the park, the cue for their daughter to stand up and jump out of the wagon like she did every week. She made a beeline to the jungle gym.

Deborah and Peter chuckled, following slowly behind. Watching her clamber up the wooden ladder, they stopped to spread out their picnic blanket so they could sit down to watch their girl play. As they sat down, their focus returned to the jungle gym.

"Where is she?" Peter asked Deborah.

"She must be hiding in the tube slide."

They laughed and held hands, walking over to the jungle gym.

"Peek-a-boo, princess!" her mother called out from a few metres away. But they heard no giggling and no little girl came running to jump into her arms. Deborah hoped their daughter was somehow blocked from their line of sight or couldn't hear her from inside the large plastic slide. Now anxious, she ran to the tube, bent down and saw it vacant. Deborah's heart pounded out of her sweater, a frantic wave spreading through her every pore.

Their daughter was not at the play equipment. Peter and Deborah turned, scouring the park in every direction. There were few trees to hide behind. Their hearts were sinking into their stomachs, desperation flooding their minds. They'd heard stories from the Dark Years and before, of people who'd kidnap children for various reasons, but this activity was unheard of in recent years. Deborah's phone rang on the blanket intended for their relaxing lunch. Peter rushed over, looking at the screen as he grasped the phone. Unknown caller. He turned on the device but didn't speak.

"Mr. Lucas. Be calm," came the voice over the phone.

Peter knew whoever it was, they could see him.

"What have you done with my daughter!" he screamed into the phone as he circled around, scouring the area.

"Now, I said to be calm. We've taken her for evaluation."

Peter screamed into the phone. "Reynolds! You creep. You can't get away with this."

"Oh, I'm afraid we can. And we will. I have every confidence that she will score very high, like her brother. And we need more gifted children like her in our program."

"We told you, we don't want her in the program."

"What *you* want is irrelevant. As of now, she's in the program."

"Now listen here ..." Peter only got so far in his reply before he got cut off.

"NO. YOU listen! Now here's where you have a choice. You can report this to the authorities and try to make a big stink, to which nobody will care and you will never see her or your son again. She will simply go down as a little girl who ran away, never to be seen again. Your son will just disappear from all systems of record, like he never existed."

Peter obviously didn't consider that a choice, but realized Reynolds was likely correct. Nobody would believe him or Deborah if they did report it, in spite of their advanced positions in their respective companies.

"And my other choice ..."

"Accept it. You will have two gifted children in the most prestigious program in the world. Your monthly stipend will double and your status in the community will increase as well."

"I'll have to discuss it with Deborah."

"Take your time. You know how to reach me. I'm sure you'll make the right choice. For both you and your children."

Dale J. Moore

# *12* *Announcement*

Breakfast lay waiting for Justin2707 in his kitchen. He pulled his scrub top over his mop of red hair and his white t-shirt, pausing to fluff his hair with his fingers before sitting down to eat.

Four weeks since the replica studies began. No word, good or bad. Surely trials were going well or he would have received orders to analyse detected deficiencies or anomalies. The wait was agonizing, and every day was a day longer before beginning on Peach. At least he'd found time to work on some personal interest programs and catch up on some reading of other researchers' work. He popped up his FID to see what correspondences awaited. His normal correspondences were relegated below a special urgent message from UbiquiMed.

"Justin2707, congratulations on your team's recent Orchid cure. This is truly a significant achievement, and as such, UbiquiMed is holding a global news conference announcing the breakthrough."

Adrenaline coursed through his veins. Finally, he'd get to meet his team in person.

"This news conference will be held today at 14:00 hours and will also feature your parents, as well as those of your colleagues."

Justin2707 started to well up with tears. His anticipation of seeing his parents face to face overwhelmed him.

"Please be at your lab FID at 13:45 to be linked into the news conference feed in a timely manner. Your punctuality and especially well-groomed appearance is appreciated."

His heart sank. No actual meeting. Just another stupid video broadcast. Would he ever meet Chantelle0206 and enjoy the sensation of simply holding her hand? Even a handshake with Nagesh1410 would have felt nice. And his parents … well that went beyond thought, let alone words.

At precisely 13:45, his lab FID overlaid the work on his screen with the ubiquitous UbiquiMed logo. A minute later, the news conference director appeared on the FID.

"Excellent, Justin2707. So glad I don't have to send you back to groom like Nagesh1410. You can relax for a few minutes – I'll prompt you again with a minute to go. You will be able to see the news conference on the FID. You will not be required to speak during the news conference. Your audio will be muted. Please smile and cordially nod when your team is introduced. Understood?"

"Yes, ma'am."

True to her schedule, at one minute before the hour, she prompted him to sit up straight and smile.

A few moments later, the screen flipped from her face to the news conference stage. Devoid of people, only a podium, with a metallic looking UbiquiMed logo, stood at the centre of the platform. Three massive displays slowly scrolled down from above the edge of the camera view, until they hung boldly emblazoned with UbiquiMed logos that slowly kaleidoscoped colourful patterns in a synchronized rhythm. The 'We're Everywhere, For You!' slogan remained static below the dancing logos. A soft orchestrated piece of music was barely noticeable.

An unseen narrator's voice came up as the music faded.

"Please welcome UbiquiMed chairman, CEO, and founder, Arthur Antonelli."

Polite applause greeted Mr. Antonelli during his trek to the podium. The camera panned over the audience, filled with reporters focused on their electronic notebooks. None of them were clapping, so the applause was piped in like the music.

"Thank you, America. You've known UbiquiMed as the world leader in providing universal health care for Americans."

Justin2707 just thought how dumb that sentence actually sounded.

"You've trusted us to care for your loved ones in our clinics, our hospitals, our sunset centres, and our medicines. And today ... well, today is a truly historic day. I am pleased ... no, overjoyed ... to announce that we are introducing Orchid, our breakthrough injection that cures testicular cancer. Yes, folks. You heard me right. It *cures* testicular cancer – not just delays the onset or slows the progression. It cures it."

Even though they weren't on screen, you could hear the chatter of the reporters and the excitement. The bottom of the FID broadcast repeated the same tag line, 'Orchid cure found!'

"And I am pleased to present to you our first two successful patients, along with their families. Mr. Alan Lee, his wife Debbie, and children Sonya and Tommy. And also, Mr. Arnie Hampton, his wife Bobbie, and daughter Wendy."

Mr. Antonelli clapped, watching the families come on stage. He walked over to greet each of them with a handshake or hug.

"Mr. Lee. Please tell us when you were diagnosed with testicular cancer."

"Four months ago, sir."

"And how were conventional treatments going?"

"The cancer was progressing. I was given two months to live. I was advised to get my personal affairs in order." His eyes teared up as he put his arm around his wife Debbie.

"And what happened two weeks ago?"

"I received an injection of Orchid. After just four hours, the doctors completed a new set of scans, and miraculously the cancer was gone!"

The murmurs in the audience grew louder. Hands shot up, but the mediator asked them to hold their questions.

"Mr. Hampton. Please tell us your story."

"Well, Mr. Antonelli, it was fairly similar. I don't know how you did it, and I really don't care." He put one arm around his wife and the other around his daughter. "All I know is that I would not be here today, in front of God and all these witnesses, if it were not for your cure."

"Thank you both, Mr. Lee and Mr. Hampton, for your courage and honesty. I would like you to be the first to meet the scientists behind this medical breakthrough of our lifetime!"

Justin2707 could see his face come up on the centre large FID, with Nagesh1410 on one side and Chantelle0206 on the other.

"In the centre we have …" and abruptly the meeting arranger pre-empted Mr. Antonelli's voice.

"Smile and nod, Justin2707."

"Now your turn, Nagesh1410."

"And now you, Chantelle0206."

"Thank you. You will now be patched back into the presentation."

Mr. Antonelli continued. "These three scientists were the leads behind this cure. They worked on this cure for over three years, assisted by a team of lab technicians and the most expensive laboratory equipment ever assembled."

Justin2707 did agree with the assessment. They certainly possessed incredible machines to perform their work. The strides in the past few years alone in equipment improvements were worthy of some medical achievement award. The team could work much quicker and get back substantiated results in a fraction of the time that it took when they first started on Orchid three years ago.

He also noticed that their FIDs had stopped transmitting live pictures, and were now just showing stills captured of them smiling. Curious, he thought.

The presentation continued.

"And we'd like to present to you the parents behind these geniuses."

Justin2707 watched his parents walk on stage, directly below his image on the large display. Likewise, the parents of Chantelle0206

and Nagesh1410 took position under their pictures. He was surprised to
see Chantelle's mother appeared of Asian descent. He'd never picked
that out in her.

The broadcast switched from showing each of the parents, back
to the audience, which now stood applauding for real. It was quite
remarkable to behold; he'd read that journalists were hardened,
unemotional, and often abandoned the truth for a sensational headline.
The view went back to Mr. Antonelli at the podium, obviously pleased
with the reaction of the crowd.

"Thank you very much for the kind response. I'd like to
introduce you to the parents of these fine doctors."

Then the screen switched over to the meeting organizer.

"That will be all for today. Thank you for your participation.
Please resume your regularly scheduled work activities."

"Wait …." but it was too late. She disappeared with the
transmission. His FID reverted to the report he had open before the call.

"Replay last 5 minutes of UbiquiMed announcement," he
barked to the FID.

The images were replayed. Justin2707 had been caught up in
the emotion of the presentation the first time he saw it, so happy to see
his parents standing under his picture. They looked like they were so
proud of him. It looked like his mother was crying, as well as squeezing
the stuffing out of his father's hand! He watched as the camera panned
over the audience.

"Stop. Resume after rewinding 20 seconds."

He looked beyond his mother and father. He looked beyond the
audience clapping.

"Stop! Zoom fifty percent and restart."

It had definitely been hard to see the first time, especially without the magnification. But there it was. Above the heads of his parents, and below the FID with his picture, he saw the background behind them. It didn't look like the violent, war torn country that they were told existed far away from their remote mountain research station. Trees blowing gently in the breeze. A paved path running along some water. Couples walking by, hand in hand. Joggers and bikers passing by. Something was going on. His suspicions drove his urge to find out what.

Dale J. Moore

# 13 *Word Spreads*

"Hello U S of A!" Bruce Templeton's voice boomed to start off the Such is Life show with a boisterous beginning. The camera slowly zoomed from a long-range view of Bruce and Tulio on the soundstage, into a close-up on the anchor. Ingrid was not in her usual spot to the left of Bruce.

"A few days ago, one of our favourite people, Mr. Antonelli of UbiquiMed stunned the world with the announcement of a cure for testicular cancer. We have stood first in line to criticize Mr. Antonelli in the past for some of his, well let's just say interesting, public appearances. The medical community has quickly verified Mr. Antonelli's claim, and thousands of people are scheduled for the injections, with hundreds already receiving it."

The camera panned over to Tulio.

"It truly is a miracle, Bruce. We now go live to our street walker -- I mean on-the-street reporter -- Ingrid."

The broadcast switched to Ingrid, holding a microphone and standing in front of a hospital nurses' station.

"Thanks, Tulio. I'm here at Memorial Hospital this morning." She began walking away from the nurses' station, the camera bouncing as it followed her down the hallway. "I'm about to enter the waiting room of a patient that is ready for his injection." The camera followed her into a semi-private room, with the curtain drawn around the far occupant. On the front bed sat a man that looked in his late thirties.

"So tell me, Mr. Post, are you excited about your injection?"

"Oh fur sure, Ingrid. I've gone and had this for a while and I'm a real anxious to get rid of it and get back to my farm."

As Ingrid started to ask a follow up question, a male nurse entered the room. "They're ready for you, Mr. Post. Please come this way."

"Okay. Well, Mr. Post's getting called in now, so we'll go back to our show and return in about five minutes when the injection is done. This amazing cure is that quick to work!" She stepped into the doorway and partway into the hall, hollering "Good Luck, Mr. Post!" Her attention turned back to the camera. "Back to you, Bruce!"

"Thanks, Ingrid. In a related story, we have with us Professor Bratwurst, a scientist from the little known Institute of Cancer Causing Isotopes, or ICCI for short."

The scene switched to a man dressed in a white lab coat. Bruce's voice was heard over the guest's image. "Please tell us the concern that you have with this cure."

"Well, this is not just my theory, but is also supported by Mr. Bigsby and Mr. Jazz."

"Oh, are they other ICCI scientists?"

"No, they are my two cats."

The camera showed a brief shot of Tulio, using his expressive face to look befuddled.

"So Bruce, if you were not aware, this Orchid cure consists of an injection of millions of microbots into your system that target the disease and then eliminate affected cells."

A brief bit of animation showed an injection on a person's buttocks, and little Pacman-like creatures moving very quickly through the blood stream toward the testicles. The last frame stayed on the screen behind Bruce and Tulio.

"Yes, so I hear. That visualization is very impressive."

"Well, what you don't hear is that these microbots are capable of being controlled remotely by Mr. Antonelli, and once he has injected enough subjects, he will turn them into an army controlled by him!"

"That's fascinating! But if the microbots go directly to your testicles, how can your brain be controlled?" Bruce inquired.

Tulio followed up with a possible explanation. "Well, Bruce, you've heard of men's actions being driven by their ..." He was cut off by Professor Bratwurst.

"What you'll see on this next piece of animation will explain."

Another brief animation piece ran, showing a few of the microbots detouring up toward the brain.

"So as you see, a handful of these little monsters are engineered to go to your brain. There they will lie dormant until UbiquiMed issues the command sequence to activate them."

The screen showed a picture of a leering Mr. Antonelli, holding an oversized remote control, with a big red button that said "Kill" on it.

"Wow. That's quite the accusation. What kind of proof do you have?"

"Well, none right now, but we believe it's just a matter of days before we have some, right, Mr. Bigsby?" The scientist turned to his cat.

"Okay… Thank you for your time." Bruce kept a straight face while Tulio rolled his eyes and made a funny face. "We may need another opinion on that theory."

"Bruce, we have Ingrid back on the feed. I'm patching her in."

The view changed to Ingrid back on site with Mr. Post standing beside her, looking none the worse for wear.

"So, how'd it go, Mr. Post?"

"I feel better already, Ingrid. I haven't felt this good in months. As a matter of fact, I think I'll do a little jig to celebrate." He started to dance up and down in his hospital robe, but suddenly bent down, grabbing at his crotch.

"What's the matter, Mr. Post?" Ingrid put her free hand on the man's shoulder.

"I think they fell off!"

"What fell off?" The camera panned from Ingrid to Mr. Post, then down to the floor. "Are those your testicles lying on the floor, Mr. Post?"

"I think they are…"

"Well, a small price to pay for your health, I should think. Back to you, Bruce".

The camera showed a split screen. One side had Bruce sitting with his jaw hanging down and Tulio squirming with his legs crossed. The other side showed Mr. Post still doubled over, trying to pick himself, or parts of himself, off the floor.

"Okay. I think we've run out of balls, I mean time, for today. We'll see you tomorrow on …"

"Such is Life!" as the second split screen now showed Ingrid so that all three actors displayed on screen.

"And Cut! Great show again, team!"

Stage hands came up from behind Bruce and Tulio, removing their lapel microphones. The two announcers pushed back from the news desk as Ingrid emerged from a door at the side of the soundstage. She came from the adjoining set that housed the show "Doctor Ann." Tulio approached her, giving her a hug, more than a casual entertainer-phony embrace.

"See you in twenty minutes?" he asked her, giving her the usual time to get out of makeup.

"Better make it twenty five. I've got to get this getup back to wardrobe too," as she pointed to the reporter trench coat and hat she'd worn for the skit.

"See you two later," Bruce briefly interrupted as he headed to his dressing room. He typically only needed ten minutes to change and get out the door, and today was no exception. He washed, changed, and headed for his transport. Sheltered from the sun, the parking lot air briskly nipped at his skin as he fumbled for his key while walking between the building and a row of new transports. Looking down as he walked, he failed to observe the two men approaching him.

"Templeton!" One of the men yelled, startling Bruce such that he jerked back slightly, keys jumping out of his hands.

"Yes…" Bruce spoke as he regained a grip on his transport keys and looked up to two unfamiliar faces.

One of the men hooked Bruce by the arm, thrusting him up against the nearby brick wall. Pinned, Bruce buckled in half as the second man stepped forward, slugging him in the gut. Bruce remained doubled over, gasping. The first man lifted Bruce's head and shoulders up just long enough for the other man to deliver a second blow.

"Now listen up. Your stories about UbiquiMed are not welcome. This visit is gentle encouragement to stop."

Bruce was in as much pain as he could remember. *This was the gentle reminder?*

"Who sent you? Antonelli?" Bruce grunted.

The man delivering the punches answered.

"Do you really think that Mr. Antonelli would even bother with a small-time broadcaster like you?"

Bruce was insulted by the small-time remark, but didn't think it time to discuss credentials and argue status with these men, considering he remained in a tight choke hold. But he did push to find his answer.

"So who did send you then?"

The man holding Bruce spoke this time; not to Bruce but to his partner.

"You shouldn't say anything more. Mr. Reynolds said to just tell him 'no more UbiquiMed jokes.' That's it. Nothing else. Then beat him up."

His partner looked at him, shaking his head.

"You're such an idiot." Then the man punched Bruce again, this time more in the ribs than the stomach. "Next time we will bust up that good looking mug of yours, and maybe a leg or arm for good measure. And if you're lucky, we'll stop there. Got it?"

"Yeah, face, limbs, got it."

Bruce was still bent over sucking wind and grimacing as one of the men pushed him hard to the ground. His pain prevented him from seeing which one did it, or really caring for that matter. They walked away without saying another word. Bruce's former mentor Roy was apparently right. He knew Reynolds was one of Antonelli's lieutenants. At least he knew who he was pissing off at UbiquiMed. Now he had to figure out how far it was worth going. After all, he liked his face the way it was. And it paid the bills.

Dale J. Moore

# *14* *Media Blackout*

In 2062, the U.S. economy and entire banking system began to fail. The U.S. government was posturing to buy out every bank in the country and consolidate into a single entity under direct control of the President. Roy Goodwyn was vehemently opposed to such a plan. He'd never taken a personal cause to air before. And after one of his rival anchors got canned for making remarks critical of the government, Roy knew that he shouldn't – but also knew he had to.

Rumours swirled of a presidential order for the military to step in to invoke the emergency broadcasting system – for an indefinite period of time. Roy didn't like big government, due to the cost and waste. Federal intervention in public and private affairs had not concerned him until now. He wasn't sure if it felt more like communism or a dictatorship, but it didn't feel much like democracy.

Sitting in his office writing his speech, a familiar face popped in the door. Bruce Templeton – Roy jokingly called Bruce his young apprentice, while Bruce responded with 'yes, Jedi Master.'

"Ready for lunch?" Bruce asked.

Saving his file and locking his computer, Roy stood up and slipped on his suit coat. "What is it now, five years?"

"Tomorrow will be five years."

"From fact finder to story writer. That's pretty good progress in this business, Bruce."

"In comparison to your turtlesque race up the corporate ladder, yes, it's meteoric. So when do I get my chance at an anchor spot?"

Roy had heard this question before. He motioned to his student to hold on for a minute, not wanting to discuss it with the other elevator occupants. They remained silent crossing the street to a deli. Now too loud to talk as they waited in line, the conversation resumed after exiting the small restaurant in search of a place to eat. Around the corner, and a few steps into the alley, Roy finally answered.

"I had plans to put you on a desk in a few weeks. Weekend stuff, early mornings. Nothing big, but a comfortable way to start."

"So why not?"

Roy chewed a small bite of his sandwich, looking around. Swallowing, he replied quietly, "Listen," he nervously looked around, "I think the whole industry is going in the tank. The feds are moving in."

"Seriously?"

"Yes," Roy firmly replied. "I'm guessing next week, maybe sooner. I think the last thing you need is to be known as a broadcaster on a major network. We are going to take the fall. We'll be called irresponsible journalists, stirring up the people to revolt. Somehow they'll even blame the impractical and un-safeguarded bank practices on the media. The banks learned nothing from the early 2000's, except how to blame others and get the government to bail them out."

"I don't need protecting! I'm not a kid, Roy," Bruce protested.

"You bet your ass you need protecting!" Roy fired back, looking around after raising his voice. "I'm expecting you to lead the media back following this shutdown. Well, not you personally maybe, but you and your peers. Lord knows if I'll have any clout when this is over – if I'm still alive."

"As if they'd knock you off. You're the second most famous broadcaster there is." Bruce knew Roy was number one, but couldn't resist the jab.

Roy smiled at the comment, but replied, "I'm not so sure. Especially after tonight."

"What's tonight?"

"My anti government-becoming-the-bank speech. We're recording it this afternoon."

"Who's we?"

"Myself, Mark Stanton, and Jill Montgomery."

"Wow. The top anchors of the top three networks. That's big. But won't your speech just push the government to quicker action?"

"It wouldn't if we were still living in a true democracy, now would it?"

"I suppose not. So what happens after your speech?"

"Don't know. But sometimes the cause is important enough and impacts so many people that you just have to take a stand while you still can." Roy started writing on the back of a business card he'd pulled from his pocket. "Here's a new email address to reach me at. Don't use it for at least a month, and then only use it from a new email address you setup. Don't use any names. I'll know it's you. Speak in riddles that you and I will know, but aren't easily deciphered." Roy handed Bruce the card, shook his hand, and held onto it for a few moments. No goodbyes were said.

Roy and the other broadcasters settled in behind a semi-circular table for taping their anti-government taping. Roy had written all the parts, and each person made a few minor edits to reflect their personal style. They were united on the message.

"Good evening, America. I'm Roy Goodwyn, and with me are Mark Stanton and Jill Montgomery. Tonight we stand united as journalists. The quality of life in our great country has continued to deteriorate over the past few years. During the last great recession, many of us learned our lessons on personal fiscal responsibility, some of us did not, and many of us have unwittingly been dragged back down the hole by the ruthless and reckless practices of our banking industry. As jobs continue to go abroad, it is easier to fall into that hole, lured by promises of a way out by an industry that knows no way out itself, except at the hands of our government."

Mark Stanton took over. "Our mission tonight is to provide you, the hard working American public, information on the state of your country. The banks are on their way down again. Once again the government will bail them out. Once again the government will not bail you out. This time, however, our sources inside the highest ranks of the government indicate that the banks will be folded into a single entity by the President. After achieving stability, he will release the banks to many of their former owners. Some smaller banks will no longer exist. Our sources indicate that the large bank owners will be forgiven all debts and violations, and all high level executives will continue to draw salaries during their temporary relief from duty. In our opinion, all this accomplishes is to place the accountability and burden of debt on the government, while letting those responsible enjoy a paid vacation." The camera switched to the third host, Jill Montgomery.

"I'm sure you're thinking, where does this leave the average, hard-working, laid off, or unemployed American worker? Still in debt, but now to the government. How will the government bail out the banks, and pay these executives to sit idly? By increasing taxes to those still lucky enough to be employed. It is a vicious downward spiral. It is the wrong approach to a serious problem. You and I are being punished, not the people responsible by their inappropriate actions. I've spoken with many of you over the past few months in a special series that I broadcast recently. I've watched you as, tears in your eyes, you've wondered how you will feed your children. The lineups at the missions and soup kitchens start early in the day, with food running out before the line does. This solution by the government is not the right one. It does not fix the problem." Jill Montgomery paused, staring forlornly into the camera. "Back to you, Roy."

"Not only does it not fix the problem, but it threatens to take away civil liberties that we hold dear. This will be the tip of the iceberg, ladies and gentleman. The tip! It is a slippery slope from this point forward. We are already hearing that the President is readying motions to take control of all public and private media outlets. We will not be living in a democracy any more, ladies and gentlemen. Lower the flag and call us Cuba! Remember Castro? Remember Stalin? It's time to stand up, people. Don't let your freedom be taken away. They will say that they are doing what they are doing to protect your freedom. It will be a lie. Don't be part of the lie. Stand up for yourselves. Stand up for your country."

The camera pulled back to show all three broadcasters. In unison, they repeated, "Fight the lies! Fight the lies! Fight the lies!"

The broadcast was met with extreme prejudice by the government. Since the entire message lasted just five minutes, the government couldn't pull it before the whole segment had aired simultaneously on all three networks. Raids on the three networks also came too late. The three anchors, their producers, and their families had all vanished earlier that evening.

As predicted, the government stepped in and took over the banks. Nothing was solved. As predicted, the government stepped in and took over the networks. Nothing was controlled. As predicted.

# 15 *Searching*

A few uneventful days slid by since the announcement of his team's Orchid cure. Justin2707 rehashed the experience in his head over and over, while trying to stay productive at his job. There were very high expectations on his team, as well as other teams, since the conclusive results. The company produced a schedule of related cures, with one release planned for every six months. He never felt that science could be put on a timetable, but management is management and not scientists.

In his mind, he calculated that his team alone could quite possibly produce a cure and verification every three months. He based his opinion on the architecture of the Orchid cure. Other UbiquiMed teams had taken different approaches to finding the Orchid cure, but those had shown mixed results. Justin was not convinced these quickie cures would be viable long-term due to some of the instabilities and side effects of the drugs produced. Trials by the other teams supported his theories. Justin preferred his team's approach as it laid a remarkable foundation for other related cancer cures. He believed the transportability of the cure to other cancer research was essential, and he would not yield from this approach when possible short cuts presented themselves during their testing. His team concurred.

He wondered why the news conference failed to explain the foundational approach and timetable. Maybe the details were discussed after his feed abruptly got cut off. Perhaps UbiquiMed didn't want to get the hopes up of so many victims, then deliver disappoint instead of a cure. He would have thought this without prejudice a few days ago. Now he thought there were motives other than the betterment of mankind.

"Nagesh1410," he spoke into his FID, requesting a link to him.

"Yes, Justin2707."

"Can you just call me Justin?"

"But Justin2707 is your name?"

"It's too long to say."

"But I know a Justin1909 too."

"Do you ever talk to us at the same time?"

"No …"

"Then just call me Justin."

"Okay Justin27 … I mean Justin"

"Thanks. Say, I've got a slight headache and feel tired, so I'm going to take something and rest for an hour or two."

"Okay. Let me know when you're back."

Justin heard a beep in the kitchen area and headed there. A headache solution appeared in a glass on the bar. He thought to himself that he'd better take it, even though he didn't really have a headache.

He just wanted some time to go offline to see if he could snoop around the UbiquiMed network outside of his normal access boundaries.

He continued working on a rogue program to find out more about his parents. He figured that UbiquiMed had to have some information on other files somewhere. So far he'd only gotten one file which showed all of his test scores going back to age three years old.

What he learned allowed him to get outside the assigned access rules. Justin also found out that the system sent a log every five minutes to the UbiquiMed master host system, limiting his searches to five minute increments. He'd just finished creating a fake log that he used to cover the tracks of where his searches had taken him. He developed an intercept program that would send his fake log at the desired time. He didn't want to use it repeatedly though for fear of getting caught. He felt comfortable sending the fake log once every hour or two.

As a result of the Orchid conference, he decided to change the focus of his search. He now wanted to find out two things: where was this UbiquiMed facility located, and what was the world *really* like outside? He knew the UbiquiMed teachings of the world were off the mark. He didn't know how different though.

"Enable keyboard and disable voice prompter," he spoke anxiously into his FID. Quite accustomed to the voice prompter, surprisingly his keyboard skills weren't bad. His nerves were showing as it took him three attempts to correctly type 'Initiate timer, upper right.' A small clock timer registered in the upper right of his FID and started counting from 00:00, in minutes and seconds. Now he knew when to send his log overlay.

'Initiate boundary expand,' he typed, this time without error. His heart rate jumped. He felt the discomfort of perspiration under his arms. He designed this routing to route him into the UbiquiMed master host system. He had limited access on the system, but at least he was in. He spent the next four plus minutes trying to expand his access rights. He made some progress, but the timer approached five minutes.

His fingers plucked 'Initiate log resend' on the keyboard, with twenty seconds to spare. He wanted to make sure that he had time to retype it if needed. 'End timer.' 'Enable voice prompter.' Then he spoke the final command "Disable keyboard."

Justin repeated this entire process seven times over the next ten hours. He gained access to a multitude of files and even other systems. He'd created a secondary ID before adding some encryption to avoid detection and tracing. If he wasn't successful, he'd find out soon enough. The day had been a tiring one, as the secrecy drained his nerves and energy. He decided to resume the next morning, but not before a quick note to his parents. He now assumed all his correspondences were scrutinized by UbiquiMed prior to being sent. So he kept it brief.

"Thanks for being at the ceremony the other day. You looked good, like the weather. See you in a few days."

It didn't even feel like he'd slept before he awoke at the same time as every other day. He performed the morning rituals and started a simple experiment before turning his focus to searching. He'd opened enough security doors in the system yesterday that he could start seeing today what information lay out there.

He initiated a search on UbiquiMed locations. A list of four hundred and eighty four floor layouts came up. He'd found his way into a facilities system. Justin narrowed it down to twenty by looking for research facilities, then to four by searching for cancer research. He copied the plans to the West facility, assuming his site to be in the western United States, since he could see tall snow capped mountains. There weren't many mountains that high in the US East, South, or Midwest, at least from what he could recall. The weather was too temperate for Alaska. He scribbled down the directory location so he could go right back on his next loop through.

In the next hour, he went back to the facility site and found links to systems that looked to control the electrical, mechanical, environmental, and water systems. His access appeared sufficient to get him into all of these systems. Today though, he'd exhausted his time. Falling behind on some experiments, as much as his mind dwelled on finding out more, he risked exposure if he didn't get caught up. His team deserved more from him as well.

Dale J. Moore

# *16* *Fame*

Deborah and Peter Lucas had begun living the good life. Not that their lives were bad before the Orchid announcement; they were taken to another level of good.

"What's on the calendar for tomorrow, hon?" Peter took off his new, expensive suit coat, as Deborah stood in front of a large mirror removing her earrings.

"We have to go to New York to be on The Morning Show the next day."

"You mean the one with Ken Walton and Shirley Hunter?"

"That's the one. They've got us down for ten minutes. Famous doctors only get fifteen minutes, you know."

"I'm surprised they fly us out there, put us up in a hotel and feed us, just to be on their show for ten minutes."

"You forgot the gifts."

"What gifts?" Peter asked, thinking his wife had changed the conversation in mid sentence again.

"They also give us gifts for appearing."

"Amazing. These celebs have got it tough, don't they?"

"That's for sure. I could get used to this!"

Almost as if it sensed the break in the conversation, the FID in the bedroom materialized and spoke: "Incoming message."

"Identify caller," Deborah spoke in response.

"The office of the President."

"Of UbiquiMed?" asked Deborah.

"Of the United States of America."

"Oh shit… I mean, please answer," replied Deborah. She was so startled she didn't realize that she stood in front of the FID with only her bra and panties on.

"Hello, Mrs. Lucas. I'm Oliver Jones. Mrs. Patterson's personal assistant." He looked at her, his eyes shifting down from her face.

Deborah finally realized her state of dress and tried crossing her arms over her chest, which only had the effect of making her breasts bulge out more from her bra. Not the effect she was going for. Peter noticed the predicament and wrapped a robe over her shoulders (and she says he doesn't notice anything!).

"Oh, yes. Very nice to meet you, Mr. Jones. To what do we owe this honour?" she said, regaining her composure now that she was clothed.

"The President would like to host you and your husband, as well as the parents of the rest of your son's team. How is 19:00 hours, day after next? We hear that you will be in New York already, so we can send transportation to get you here from there."

"Are you kidding …" Peter could be heard in the background, off screen from view of Oliver Jones.

"Of course we'll be there."

"Excellent! We will contact you shortly after you arrive in New York to finalize the arrangements. These things do sometimes get cancelled on short notice."

"I'm sure. Maybe we'll have a better offer …" Deborah joked.

Mr. Jones did not look impressed as he ended the call.

"Are you crazy?" Peter asked, after making sure the FID turned off. *"Maybe we'll have a better offer?"*

Deborah waltzed over to him, letting her robe drop to the ground behind her. "I have a better offer for you right now…"

The uneventful flight to New York did not tire them as one would expect, going coast to coast and losing time. A limo transport awaiting their arrival promptly whisked them off to a new hotel designed to look like an old European castle. Peter was quite sure that no European castle, even before the Dark Years, ever had such elegance and extravagance. Certainly 'every suite contains a hot tub and simulated lap pool' exceeded the luxury of an eight-hundred year-old castle. They enjoyed every amenity as they relaxed the night before their Morning Show appearance. They knew the interview would be brief, so they didn't think much about preparing answers like they had for prior local interviews. Besides, Deborah had them practise so much the last few times that neither felt the necessity to rehearse.

The next morning came quickly. It wasn't that they'd stayed awake late, or consumed too much alcohol, but all that relaxation had fatigued them. They got dressed in their best outfits, each taking turns helping the other. Peter needed help with his cuff links, and Deborah with the zipper on the back of her dress.

**95**

The broadcast recording took place in the building adjacent to the hotel, meaning a simple traverse of the third floor crosswalk to enter the studio. Just as well, thought Peter, with the rain that morning. They were greeted politely at reception, and an assistant to the show escorted them to a dressing room for makeup. Deborah was a little put off by the additional makeup, implying to her she was incapable. Peter assured her that the lighting made it necessary, and it had nothing to do with her appearance or ability to do her own makeup. It seemed like only a few minutes until they were situated at the side of the stage waiting for their introduction. In actuality, almost two hours had passed. The studio flowed with electric activity, as all hands prepared for the upcoming show. Time flew by for the Lucases as they soaked it all in.

"Our next guests are Deborah and Peter Lucas. Who are these people, you may ask." Ken smiled and turned to Shirley.

"Yes, Ken, they certainly aren't household names. Let me show you this brief clip for those of you who need a hint." The screens around the studio started to play a brief clip of the Orchid press conference, which included Mr. Antonelli introducing the Lucases. The clip ended, followed by a round of applause that delayed Ken continuing.

"Please continue your applause and welcome Deborah and Peter Lucas to the Morning Show!" Ken motioned to the side of the stage where they stood. Deborah and Peter walked out, looking at the audience and nodding. The size of the audience exceeded previous experiences and what they'd anticipated, leaving them both a little star struck. Deborah glanced at Peter and squeezed his hand tight for reassurance. They sat in the chairs on the right, as instructed off stage.

Ken always occupied the seat to the left to take advantage of his 'good side.' Deborah nervously tapped her fingers on Peter's knee, until he grasped her hand to calm her. His nerves bested him as well, but it wasn't outwardly apparent. His insides though were on a roller coaster ride.

Sensing her nervousness, Ken directed his first question to Peter.

"Peter, tell us how you felt standing on that stage, hearing that your son led the team that cured testicular cancer. It must have felt amazing!"

"It was, Ken. Deborah and I talked afterward. We both felt like we were ten feet off the ground. I'm glad the camera didn't catch it, but I was crying."

"You were crying?" asked Shirley. "What about you, Deborah, were you crying too?"

"Yes I was, but if there was a joy metre, I would have broken that."

"That's a good one, Deborah. Maybe we should get a joy metre here on the show."

Shirley had opened the door to asking Deborah questions. Now she hit her with a hard one, right out of the blue.

"Deborah, many people may not know this, but your son joined the UbiquiMed program at an early age. Most parents feel anxiety over a teenager moving away to go to college. You must be pretty heartless to ship off a young boy like that."

Deborah, Peter, and Ken all sat stunned by the serious turn in the course of the interview. The Morning Show had a reputation as a light, fluffy, get-your-morning-rolling, feel-good kind of show. It was not a hard-hitting journalistic show.

Peter interjected, though still in as much shock as Deborah about the question. "It was a gut wrenching decision that we made together," although Peter knew better. "We knew that UbiquiMed could provide an education unrivalled on the planet. We also hoped that someday he and others in this program would produce this kind of benefit for mankind."

"Isn't that a little egotistical to think that 'my child is going to save the world,' when he is three?" Shirley continued with the aggressive questioning. It already bothered Peter, so he decided to use his answer to retaliate.

"Perhaps. But if you were a parent, you'd know that is the hope of every parent for their child." This hit a sore spot for Shirley, as her inability to bear children was well publicized.

Ken knew he had to lighten things up, and jumped in to change the direction of the conversation.

"So, Deborah, what's next for your amazing doctor son? Which cancer is next on his radar screen? We're all anxious to know!"

"Well, Ken, we don't know. Peter and I are more excited about him getting out of the program in two months so we can help him establish his own research company or private practice."

"Two months?" Ken looked at her, puzzled.

"Two months and three days to be precise," she replied. Peter grinned in support.

"I thought the students were in the program until age twenty-five?"

"That's right, Ken."

"But Justin is only twenty-three …" Ken then noticed a cut-to-commercial motion from his director and a quick cue to segue to the next segment. "Well, that's interesting. Speaking of interesting, after this short break we'll be back with a surprise guest. Stick around to see who it is – you may not believe who's stopping by!"

Deborah and Peter were ushered off stage as the crew made some set adjustments in preparation for the next guest. Both were confused. With the attack by Shirley still on their minds, now they also had this age issue popping up. They discussed it briefly in the dressing room as the show's staff removed their makeup. They gave up trying to talk during the makeup removal process, their faces being assaulted mid-sentence. Deborah then had to re-apply her own makeup. As she did so, Peter's phone rang. It was Oliver Jones, alerting the Lucases they had twenty minutes to get to the hotel lobby or they would miss their ride to Washington. Deborah scooped her makeup items into her purse and off they went to the crosswalk back to the hotel.

"Why do you think Ken and Shirley think Justin is twenty-three?" Shirley asked as they walked-jogged through the crosswalk.

"I'm not sure, but I'd say UbiquiMed included something in a press release."

"But why lie about his age?"

"Money of course. If they can keep him in the program for two more years, any additional cancer cures are property of UbiquiMed. Look at lineups and demand for this cure. Who knows how much money this cure is generating for them? They'll throw this enormous cheque at us and expect us to grab it like we've won the lottery."

They spotted Oliver in the lobby, standing much shorter in person than he'd appeared on the FID. He directed them to a nearby elevator where the hotel manager inserted a key into the lock, enabling their vertical chariot to ascend to the roof exit. They emptied out of the elevator, through a heavy steel door to the roof, where a private transport waited, engines running. The presidential seal tattooed the transport. Now Deborah and Peter were impressed.

The ride to Washington was uneventful from the pilot's vantage point. It was anything but from the Lucas' perspective. The limo from the day before had been more luxurious, but somehow this transport made them feel more regal. Perhaps the personal airspace provided by the three armed transport escort had something to do with it. Nothing says 'I'm important' more than a military escort. Peter wondered if self-importance and status were the real reasons why celebrities surrounded themselves with bodyguards, and not actual protection.

Their route ventured a few downtown airspaces where normally no transports travelled above one hundred feet. The spectacular view had Deborah once again holding Peter's hand tightly. This time, however, a smile presided over her face, not a look of fear.

Oliver accompanied them in the presidential transport, but sat silently during the flight. As they landed, the transport engines dimmed, and Oliver addressed them.

"The meet and greet has moved up to 15:00 hours, due to other developments. The Lees and the Krishnamurthys are already here."

Peter and Deborah had met the other parents on stage, but limited to the same manner as the broadcast audience. No personal introductions occurred after the event, so they knew nothing about each

**100**

other. Peter and Deborah couldn't even agree upon the first names that they'd heard during the announcement. They agreed not to argue about it further. Likely neither of them got their counterparts' names right in the excitement.

Oliver escorted them into a room containing the other parents, and fortunately did another round of introductions.

"Debbie and Michael Lee, this is Deborah and Peter Lucas. And this is Kamala and Pradeep Krishnamurthy."

Peter and Deborah looked at each other with a grin -- neither of them had remembered the names correctly.

Oliver put a couple of fingers up to his right ear as he received a message on his earpiece. He then returned his attention to the six parents.

"This is strictly a meet and greet. It is a photo opportunity for the president and an acknowledgement of your children's success. The only questions will come from the president herself. A short, polite answer is expected. You will not be allowed to ask any questions of the president, even if she asks you if you have any questions. You will be allowed to ask one question per couple before you meet the president. Her staff or I will respond within 24 hours. Keep in mind that the response may be 'no response.' Please acknowledge that you understand these directions by repeating "I understand" as I look at each one of you. Oliver looked each person in the eyes, and nodded upon receipt of their vocal response.

"Okay, now that the formal instruction is over, please accept my apology for my direct nature. Just keep in mind that you are about to meet the most powerful person in the world. Her time is extremely valuable. I am blessed to receive an occasional five minutes alone with the president to just talk about life. She is an incredible person. That she is taking fifteen minutes out of her schedule to meet you speaks volumes about what your children have achieved."

As a long-time admirer of the President, even before she ran for office, Deborah's heart pounded with expectation. The President was a rare common vote for Deborah and Peter.

Peter took a pen and a piece of paper from Oliver to write their one question. The Lees and Krishnamurthys were still discussing what to write when Peter handed the paper to Oliver, who looked quite surprised to get it back so soon.

"Peter, this isn't a question," and Oliver started to hand it back to him.

Deborah didn't even look at what Peter had written, but knew.

"No, it's not. But it's a truth that needs to be known."

The meeting with the President was everything Deborah had hoped for. The personable nature of the President made them at ease, like they'd known her forever. Impressive for a fifteen minute meet and greet, Peter would say later. She presented each of the families with a plaque of appreciation from the Office of the President of the United States of America. She asked them if they had any questions. They all followed instructions and politely said 'No, thank you.' The memorable, once in a lifetime experience stood head and shoulders above the unpleasant episode on The Morning Show from earlier in the day. The President departed, escorted by her secret service agents, rushing off to something more important than a meet and greet. But for those fifteen minutes, she made it sound just as important to the Lees, Krishnamurthys, and Lucases.

Dale J. Moore

# 17 *Missing Years*

Fresh off of his beating in the parking lot, Bruce Templeton wanted to downplay verbal assaults on UbiquiMed today. Part of him remained angry about the intimidation from the UbiquiMed thugs; he wanted to rip into them and their leader Mr. Antonelli. But his ribs told him that maybe a less aggressive approach was a good option for right now. So Bruce, who had lead writer authority, re-organized the story order to focus on a related story that didn't make UbiquiMed look bad. He would then do a follow-up piece on yesterday's story, but without skewering UbiquiMed. At least not too much.

"Welcome to today's show. Today, in the best journalistic tradition of ripping off other stations, we're going to eat up some of our thirty minutes that we have to fill by showing clips from other shows," Bruce led into the story.

"This cuts down on the time that we need to spend writing each day. And let's face it – we are lazy," a wise-cracking Tulio followed.

"So let's see this clip from The Morning Show this morning," Ingrid said, turning to watch a monitor to her side. The clip showed the Lucases discussing Justin's age on the show.

"Well, Bruce," continued Ingrid. "I'm not a mother ..."

"Well that's your opinion," interrupted Tulio.

"As I was saying, I'm not a parent, but don't you think that you should be able to keep track of your own kid's age?" she finished, this time uninterrupted.

"Perhaps they're right?" a dubious Tulio asked, using his well-worn confused look.

"Well, I've just so happened to get my hands on copies of Justin Lucas's birth record. Can we show this on the screen?" Bruce laid out a document on the desk for the camera operator to zoom in for a close-up shot.

Ingrid added, "Now I'm not a math major, Bruce, but even I can tell you that this shows that he is almost twenty-three, not almost twenty-five."

"So what gives?" Tulio asked. "How can one of the brightest minds in the world today have parents that are as dumb as a stick?"

"Well, I guess that separation at age three might have something to do with it. But let's go with the dumb as a stick theory for now," Bruce concluded.

"During yesterday's report, we interviewed a Professor Bratwurst about his robotic army of microbots." Tulio appeared split-screen with an image from yesterday's interview, showing the professor rubbing one of his cats. "Today we learned that the gentleman we interviewed was not a scientist as we were led to believe, but actually runs the Professor Bratwurst hot dog and bratwurst stand two blocks south of our building. His cats declined comment, as they were busy eating one of his foot-long dogs."

"And in another related story," Bruce reported, "Ingrid, you'll be glad to hear that there have been no additional reports of massive testicle loss after your story yesterday with Mr. Post." A picture of the de-testicled Mr. Post displayed with Ingrid looking down at the grounded jewels.

A suddenly enthusiastic Ingrid sat up in her chair. "Massive testicles ... now that would be worth seeing!"

Dale J. Moore

# 18 *Outside World*

His attempts to uncover information about the outside world had led Justin to find out about the world immediately around him. The architectural diagrams indicated that he lived in a reasonably large complex with a tunnel system below it. The tunnels branched off in various directions, with one appearing to head up the mountainside. It could just be an airshaft, but it looked larger on the blueprint.

Justin kept working in five minute increments to explore the new boundaries of his security, as well as to expand his access further. He came upon the internal FID mail routing system, and almost gave it no additional thought. After all, there was nothing unusual about the setup. There were no extra security layers on top of it to indicate it held anything worth viewing. He was just about to leave the directory, when he noticed the directory size. He toggled over to his email folder on his system. The newly discovered directory had a new file for today that did not exist on his system's email. Definitely an anomaly worth investigating.

He flipped back and accessed the new email. A message popped up on his FID.

'Hey, Doctor Justin Lucas. Just wanted to say congrats and thanks for your Orchid cure. It saved my Dad's life. You're the best! Dan Peterson. P.S. I hope you saw the latest 'Such is Life' broadcast. If not, here's a link.'

"Justin Lucas!" he exclaimed out loud. He'd never known his last name. He'd only heard his name as Justin, and not Justin2707, a few times. And only when he begged Nagesh1410 to say it that way.

He absolutely needed to try the link. He copied it to a file, down to a couple of minutes of his five, and planned a return to this site again later with a full five minutes. Justin executed the link, starting a broadcast of a show entitled 'Such is Life,' a news telecast. "Welcome to today's show. Today, in the best journalistic tradition of ripping off other stations …" The clip continued for another thirty seconds or so before showing a brief glimpse of Justin's parents.

And then the transmission was lost. Justin frantically started typing 'Initiate log resend.' The log was no sooner sent than a message came across the FID.

"You have accessed an ancient archived show from the Dark Years. We terminated the transmission for your protection. UbiquiMed Security Division."

He knew they obviously were lying about this being an archived show, since he saw his parents in it and their age looked current. The email itself referred to him by name – Justin Lucas. Now that he knew who he was, he needed to find out more. Tomorrow he would try the link again.

The next day couldn't come soon enough for him, although he did stick to routine and planned to awake at his regular time. He didn't want to attract any undue attention, as he wondered how much of his life came under constant surveillance.

.

Dale J. Moore

# 19 *Security*

The years leading the Child Mental Assessment division were rewarding to Solomon Reynolds. He personally was responsible for recruiting the cream of the crop of the five hundred-plus scientists in the program today. He did not shy away from boasting about his accomplishments to Mr. Antonelli. Solomon felt the processes were well established for finding and procuring additional scientific assets, so this work now lay beneath his attention.

Solomon's sights set on his next position, he developed a plan to aggressively obtain the job. He went to great lengths to discredit the director in charge of scientific research. A very competent scientist, he ran a tight department, and was a good man. But the Research Director stood in the way. Solomon went out of his way to become friends with the man, gaining his trust by appearing as a supporter of the man and his department. There were documented instances when Solomon stood up in executive meetings rallying behind the man for equipment or other funding requests.

Visiting the labs on a few occasions after midnight, Solomon deliberately sabotaged experiments and the associated documentation. Influenced by his friend Solomon, the director became convinced someone inside his department was tampering with the experiments. When no evidence to support this theory materialized, Antonelli and the executive board began to look for another explanation. Confidence waned in results produced from the labs. After repeated attempts to rectify the problem proved unsuccessful, after repeated nefarious deeds by Solomon, an outside security and auditing firm was brought in to investigate. All departmental resources were questioned, as well as all other directors. Due to his staunch support of the director and the research department on many occasions, Solomon's questioning was a formality. The one hundred and ninety-six page final report focused on poor controls in place for the Research department, identifying thirty-one instances of carelessness or recklessness. Mr. Antonelli ordered almost an entire year of research, by hundreds of scientists, to be discarded in its entirety. The department sat in shambles and the director's reputation was irrevocably damaged. The Research department found itself without a director.

Solomon Reynolds came forward two days later with a brilliantly crafted analysis and presentation that covered every specific issue experienced over the past six months, tying neatly to the final report. This of course was easy for him, since he had created most of the problems in the first place. The few that he didn't create were, by any measurement, insignificant as individual items, but provided good cover for those manufactured by Solomon. Mr. Antonelli gave Reynolds the job on the spot, bestowing upon him the new title of Director of Research and Controls. Part of the presentation included a shift of focus for research from air borne illnesses to cancer research. Solomon Reynolds was no great humanitarian – he simply saw massive

**114**

wealth in developing cures for cancer. Cancer was a major cause of death years earlier, but experienced a drastic escalation since the Dark Years and the use of nerve gases to control an unruly population. Some sort of cancer now affected one in two people by age forty, and two in three by age fifty-five. Who wouldn't want a product that could be sold to that many people? Besides, he approached the age where his odds were going to start shrinking, and as always, Solomon looked out for himself.

The search for cancer cures was more difficult than Solomon Reynolds initially thought. He knew it wouldn't be easy, but he estimated within five years he'd be taking a series of cures to market. Ten years had now passed. His department had created a number of blockers which effectively slowed many cancers down. These blockers were very profitable to UbiquiMed, earning him a promotion to Associate Vice President.

As much as Solomon was disappointed in not having a cure, it paled in comparison to the public reaction. Mr. Antonelli manipulated the media for many years. Solomon kept the blockers coming and each new blocker pacified the press for many months. The blockers initially created public excitement, but after a few years the hype faded, transforming into resentment for UbiquiMed's lack of progress. People were still dying after all. UbiquiMed's blockers bought many people an extra year or eighteen months, but not much more. Those extra months, however, were very painful and difficult to witness by family and friends.

UbiquiMed had come under growing scrutiny in recent years for the lack of any definitive cures. Most specifically, they were criticized for not coming up with any cures with all the money provided by the federal government. Antonelli was getting old and many of his cronies had retired long ago from the media outlets, diminishing his influence from what it used to be. He also suspected information leaks coming out of UbiquiMed, prompting a full corporate security investigation.

Once again, Solomon Reynolds foresaw an opportunity and exploited it. Having created the security leaks, he came up with a plan to plug them. He convinced Mr. Antonelli that the controls and security put in place in the research department were extendable to the entire corporation. Solomon Reynolds received a promotion to Vice President of Security and Media Relations.

The security leak of course was fixed. The media uprising was managed to some extent but not contained. Solomon convinced the major media outlets to downplay the lack of final cures for a while, but the groundswell began again. The little independents were running amuck with stories. It was about to explode. Fortunately for both Antonelli and Reynolds, the Orchid cure came along. The heat from the media dissipated, replaced by praise. The coffers replenished handsomely with the cure on the market. All was well once again. And Solomon Reynolds wanted to keep it that way.

News of Justin Lucas breaching security protocols to access current broadcasts was disturbing to Solomon. As head of security, he needed to secure one of the company's greatest assets. He appreciated the intellect of Justin Lucas and knew that a fabricated story wouldn't work. It required a direct approach.

"Justin2707. I am Solomon0214. How are you today?"

"I'm fine. How are you?"

"I'm a little distressed. I am the Vice President of Security and Media Relations at UbiquiMed. It has come to my attention that you recently breached some of our security protocols."

"I was told that I stumbled across an unauthorized broadcast from the Dark Years."

"You and I both know that isn't true. As punishment for this breach, your video calls with your parents are suspended for one week. If you continue this activity, you are jeopardizing the safety of your parents. Understood?"

"Yes, understood."

"Good. Solomon0214 out."

With that taken care of, Solomon set up a meeting with Mr. Antonelli to brief him on the issue. In a review of Justin Lucas's file, Solomon found that old tracking devices remained on all of the researchers over age twenty. Mr. Antonelli argued that the flight risk was extremely low, but agreed with the recommendation to immediately update the trackers to protect their investments. The Washington office received the order for new trackers.

While he had his time, Solomon Reynolds updated his boss on their troublesome broadcaster. The warning had been issued, and he was ready to act with additional force as necessary.

**117**

Dale J. Moore

# *20* *Kidnapped*

Paranoia wasn't in Justin's thought process vocabulary. It was discomforting. In the past few days, his view of the world changed more than it had in the previous twenty years. For a person of structured routine, it unsettled him. This morning he was threatened, or at least his parents' safety was at stake. Sometimes, he admitted to himself, he took the jumpy, scrambled communications with his parents for granted. He looked forward to their daily calls – how would he survive an entire week without seeing them, or simply reading their written thoughts? He could only recall a few occasions where a day went by without some form of correspondence. But never two days in a row. How would he possibly manage seven days? He'd experienced anxiety over experiment results before, but his life – likely all the scientists' lives – was free from outside stress. His mind raced like a runaway transport. Like a dozen runaway transports, destined on a collision course. Justin's brain was his greatest asset. It was vital that he control its speed and direction. Determined not to let his fear or new emotions get the best of him, he closed his eyes and meditated.

   For the next few hours, his return to the 'Such is Life' site would have to wait. His research sat idle. It was time to catch up. He dedicated three hours to the latest analysis and experiments. Focus was paramount to complete his work properly, and while challenging, he mustered up the concentration to slow down the spiraling thoughts, pushing them into the deep recesses of his brain.

The efforts to channel his thoughts were successful. Deep into his analysis, he was still working when the FID informed him that lunch was prepared and simmering in the kitchen. He observed the time. Five hours had streamed by, his mind harnessing the adrenaline to accomplish two days of work. This progress afforded him time for a distraction after enjoying his lunch.

While eating, he scribbled down a schedule of objectives for his five-minute ventures today. He would get about five episodes today, having gone the whole morning buried in scientific research. Justin's first order of business would be development of a method to mask his trips to the 'Such is Life' site. Solomon0214's warning only made Justin more determined to figure out what was going on. He chose to write out his routine on paper first to save time in the system. This way he hoped to only use two trips on implementing his new masking routine, saving two for 'Such is Life.' The final foray was earmarked to find out about his parents. He assumed that Mr. and Mrs. Lucas had first names, and would like to know them (even if he'd never dare call his parents by their first names).

Lunch was satisfying, for its taste, removal of hunger, and the planning accomplished. He resumed his scientific analysis, but it was simply a matter of starting a few simulations – nothing that would tax his brain or newly acquired energy. The simulations would also provide cover for his other activities. Setting up monitors and reminders for the simulations, he went about putting in place his masking routine. It went very quickly, testing out well within the two planned cycles. A few hours later he set out on his first journey of the day into the new world. His new routine meant just a few seconds ticked off until successfully navigating to the site of the 'Such is Life' broadcast. He opted not to watch any more of yesterday's broadcast, instead starting today's episode.

"Good morning everyone!" The name underneath the announcer read Bruce Templeton. He sat with a bit of a hunch that wasn't apparent yesterday in the brief moments that Justin saw him. The announcer continued.

"Well, Tulio, we have a breaking news story related to UbiquiMed. Can you give us some details?"

"Certainly, Bruce! Before we go to Ingrid, who's on the scene, let's give our viewers some background information."

The broadcast went to split-screen, with Tulio on one side and a picture of Justin's parents on the other side.

"The parents of Doctor Justin Lucas have been kidnapped this morning. As you know, Dr. Lucas led the team of brilliant scientists that came up with the Orchid cure for testicular cancer. We go live now to Ingrid, who is standing outside the Lucas' home."

"Well, Tulio, it is quite the scene here. There are a few government security transports here, as well as some UbiquiMed security transports."

Bruce appeared on split-screen with Ingrid. He turned toward her and posed a question.

"Ingrid, have you heard the demands of the ransom note?"

"No, not yet, Bruce. But I have just gotten the following press release from a UbiquiMed official. I'm going to read it word for word, so bear with me as I'm just seeing this now… 'This morning, Deborah and Peter Lucas, parents of Dr. Justin Lucas, were kidnapped from their home. While the demands are not being made public at this time, there were reasons stated in the ransom note that can be revealed. The kidnapper, or kidnappers, stated that they were in line for a huge insurance claim for a terminally ill man. Unfortunately, since the Orchid cure, the man is no longer terminal and the kidnapper will not be collecting this large death benefit.'"

"That's amazing, Ingrid!" Tulio exclaimed. "I never thought about this, but there have to be thousands of spouses in this situation. Bye bye trip around the world. Your husband's going to live, so your trip will not!"

"That's for sure, Tulio," she replied. "While UbiquiMed didn't release a ransom amount, my sources say they are asking for one billion dollars!"

"Well, with all the money they are going to make on this medicine, that's a drop in the UbiquiMed bucket," Bruce chimed in.

The timer in the corner of Justin's FID was winding down. He dropped off and sent the fake log. Slumping down in the chair, he ran the fingers of both hands through his full head of red hair. He never dreamed that his parents would be kidnapped over his research. Or were they kidnapped for another reason? Had Solomon0214 stopped protecting his parents as he'd threatened? Or maybe Solomon0214 had actually arranged the kidnapping? Justin sat up, resting his elbows on his desk as he leaned forward. Tilting his head down, he placed the fingertips of each hand on the sides of his temple. He massaged his temple for a minute, not realizing he was doing it, but subconsciously trying to relieve the stress on his mind. His eyes remained closed, even after his fingers stopped their circular patterns.

Justin didn't know what to expect of the outside world. He'd been told his whole life that it was a violent, war torn place where personal freedoms were sacrificed for the good of the whole. He was completely fine with personally making that sacrifice, but the views of the Orchid conference showed a different world from the implanted version. But then his parents got kidnapped. And maybe they were kidnapped by UbiquiMed. It was certainly confusing. Justin didn't know what to expect from the outside world, but he became determined to find out, and soon.

Dale J. Moore

# *21* *Stolen Drugs*

The show started with a tale of the Lucas' kidnapping. It was well acted and blended a reality feel with enough tongue in-cheek humour to play well. Now Tulio led the second story of the day.

"We are hearing reports of the Orchid cure being re-routed."

"You mean stolen, Tulio?" Bruce asked.

"Yes, that's what I said. It's being diverted ..." Tulio rephrased his words, unfazed by the interruption.

"That's not the same as stolen?" Ingrid asked, supporting Bruce's stance.

"I suppose you could look at it that way if you were a negative person." Tulio adjusted his sitting posture, looking agitated.

"So it was stolen," Bruce matter-of-factly stated.

"Yes, Mr. Negative. It was stolen! Are you happy now?" Tulio had made himself go red to simulate anger and frustration. Daunted, he continued nonetheless.

"As I was saying, stolen batches of the Orchid cure have been selling on the black market for a pretty hefty price."

"I can imagine that there's a big demand for such a wonder drug, and that UbiquiMed is having trouble keeping up, hence driving demand to a frenzied state," summarized Bruce.

"Perhaps you will let me finish my story before you interrupt with your irrelevant theories. As I was going to say, the drug is being sold in night clubs ..."

This time he was interrupted by Ingrid, who squirmed in the chair, looking very turned-on by the discussion.

"Does it work as some sort of aphrodisiac?"

"You are on the right track, Ingrid. The drug is rumoured to have an unpublicized side effect. It gives men a multi-hour erection, and in the process increases the size of their manhood by on average three to four inches."

"I guess those microbots are amazing little fellas," Ingrid smiled from ear to ear. Her hair hung down and she twirled a long strand with her fingers, looking sexily at the camera.

"I suppose now the advertisements for Orchid are going to have to contain a disclaimer at the end, like 'may cause prolonged erection and increase in penis size' or some such thing," Tulio added.

"So, Tulio, are there any reports that your penis falls off after this prolonged state of, well, growth?" Bruce said, appearing awkward to talk about it. He continued. "After all, we had a recent story about testicles dropping off following the injections."

Ingrid, still pretending to be turned on, excitedly clicked her pen, making the tip go in and out as she tapped her other hand on the desk in front of her.

"Perhaps," she started, "this is why Mr. Antonelli has all of these young sex kittens hanging off his arm. I'm thinking the term 'a dose of his own medicine' means something completely different here."

Dale J. Moore

# 22 *Emmaline*

Bruce Templeton sat at a quaint outside café, sharing a tale of slight exaggeration with his date. His attractive, and somewhat younger companion, smiled attentively and laughed at the impressions he used to tell the story. The quiet table for two was situated off to the corner of the patio. Bruce had requested this specific table to minimize interruptions that sometimes occurred when recognized by a fan. If forced to confess, he'd have to admit he wanted the seclusion to focus on Emmaline, and only Emmaline.

To this point in his life, he remained a confirmed and content bachelor. Emmaline was starting to change his mind. He'd felt the raging hormones of lust many times before, and had had some truly spectacular and wild relationships over the years. Some of his relationships were distinctly one night (or two night) stands that usually suited both participants nicely. There'd been the occasional disgruntled partner who pursued him for more than a fling, and he'd acted similarly a few times. In all the years though, he'd only dated two women for more than three months. In both cases, compatibility didn't exist outside of sex. But the sex was so good that neither party wanted to end it. Eventually they realized it could never be anything permanent and they moved on.

Emmaline, though, was different. Hell, he thought, four dates in two weeks and he hadn't even slept with her yet. Not that he didn't want to. Something about just being with her satisfied him, albeit differently from a night of passion. He had this new sensation of not wanting to mess up. He was fascinated listening to her talk. Bruce had a habit of dominating the conversation on dates, but now found himself listening as much as talking. This too was new to him.

"I love the way you look at me when I talk," Emmaline said to him, reaching forward to hold his hand on the round wrought iron café table. "It's nice to date a guy who's looking at my eyes when I talk and not at my breasts!"

"Your eyes are very expressive. Although your breasts look quite lovely too."

She smacked his hand lightly at the comment, smiled, then took a sip of her Cabernet.

"By the way," she said, putting down her glass, "do you know the gentlemen a few tables over? They've been looking over here for the last twenty minutes."

"Perhaps they are looking at your breasts?" he quipped as he turned to look toward them. "No, I don't recognize them. Not my usual fans either, nor do they look like a couple. Shall I pay the bill so we can go for a nice walk down the boardwalk?"

"Sounds perfect to me, except let me split on the bill. I won't take no for an answer!"

They settled up their bill and Bruce threw a few extra bucks on the table where the tip lay.

"My sister's a waitress and has burned in my brain to tip heavily."

He followed Emmaline out of the café. Crossing the cobblestone road, she put her arm in his as they strolled toward the boardwalk. A store front caught Emmaline's eye so they slowed to a stop. Thank God it was closed, thought Bruce. He wasn't in the mood for browsing at purses and shoes. While she graciously leaned forward to glimpse the price of a particular purse, Bruce glanced around the street, only to be alarmed to spot the two men from earlier at the restaurant. They likewise had stopped in front of another store. They didn't look like stop-and-browse kind of guys. He now believed he was being followed.

"Well, is it worth coming back for another time?"

"The purse is, but I'm not sure the price is. Maybe I can talk them down another day."

"I wouldn't be surprised if you could persuade them to give it to you for cost, or maybe even for free!"

"I'll take that as a compliment," and she resumed holding his arm as they turned back on course for their destination. A glimpse over his shoulder revealed no sign of the two men. Perhaps his newsman instincts were getting the best of him. He told himself he was just cautiously aware of his surroundings, not paranoid.

"I just love it down here at night. It reminds me of when I was a girl. My parents were separated and on Sundays my father would bring me down here. Not always, but every so often, I'd get to stay with him

**131**

until the early evening. The boardwalk always became magical in the evening. The lights reflecting off the water. The sounds of the seals carrying across the quiet of dusk."

"I used to come down here to write when I was younger. I had a lot of time on my hands during the broadcast ban. Depending on the time of day, it was either a great place for solitude or someplace where you could just watch people."

"Oh, that's one of my favourite hobbies too! Let's play a game that my father and I used to play."

"I'm not one much for games…"

"Get over it, big guy. This game will suit you and your comedic sensibilities. Let's sit on this bench and then I'll go first." They both sat, her arm still wrapped in his, as she snuggled up against him. He closed his eyes, enthralled by the scent of her hair and the way her skin enhanced her perfume. He liked this game so far.

"Now, I'll pick out someone, or a couple, and I'll tell you where I think they are from, what they do for a living, etc. You then have to elaborate on their story. We then switch and you'll go first."

"Sounds simple enough."

"Okay. Let's see … who to start with … oh, oh, her …" and she tapped him on the leg, pointing to a lady picking bottles out of the trash can. "She's come from New York, looking for a change of pace from her executive position. She now makes a living cashing in bottles for their deposit money."

"Very good. The irony of the situation is that she used to work for the bottling company as manager of distribution. She is collecting the bottles as evidence in a lawsuit against the company for selling a product that pollutes the environment because its design leads consumers to believe that it is not a returnable bottle."

"I see. That's a little more intense than I'm used to, but let's go another round. Your turn first."

"Alright. The elderly couple at the railing over there. By the lamplight. They are here from Detroit. It's the first time they've taken a vacation in the 34 years they've been married, and the first time that either of them has seen the ocean."

Emmaline added, "And it's not an entirely happy occasion. She has terminal cancer and this is their way of saying goodbye to each other. He doesn't know it, but when they return home, she will take an overdose of pills, not able to take the pain anymore. She's also thinking of him obediently by her side as her soul and body deteriorate while she slowly dies. She doesn't want him to suffer."

"Wow. Talk about intense! You made my ending look like a fairy tale. Perhaps UbiquiMed will come up with a cure before they return home."

"I didn't picture you for an optimist, Bruce."

"Maybe you bring out the best in me." Bruce leaned toward her and began to kiss her. Just before he closed his eyes, something caught his attention. The kiss was short, and startled her by its brevity.

"What's wrong?"

"Remember those two men at the restaurant? They were following us earlier, but I thought I was just paranoid. But there they are again. Slowly look ... they're just over your right shoulder."

Turning, she recognized them.

"Who do you think they are?"

"UbiquiMed sent some goons the other day to rough me up a bit."

"Why would they do that? And why didn't you tell me?"

"I didn't want you worrying."

"Surely they won't try anything out here in the midst of everyone."

"I doubt it too, but I should get you home." They walked a block away from the men, where Bruce flagged down a transport taxi. Emmaline slid across the seat as Bruce followed her into the stopped transport. Zooming away, Bruce looked over his shoulder for a few blocks for a trace of pursuit by the men. Convinced that they weren't followed, he asked the taxi driver to stop.

"Listen. I'm going to get out and walk home from here. I'll pay the taxi for the rest of the way to get you home. I'll contact you later. Don't worry. I'll be alright." He reached forward and slid money through the slot to the driver, giving him instructions to continue to her place. He opened the door, but Emmaline pulled him back. She gave him a kiss unlike any they had shared to date. He stared longingly into her eyes, desperately wanting to go home with her, but knowing better. Bruce thought he saw tears in her eyes through the rear window of the departing taxi, but his own tears made it difficult to tell.

# 23 *The Old Apartment*

Bruce arrived at his apartment building a few minutes prior to 22:00 hours. The historic building had undergone numerous renovations over the years, before and since Bruce moved in. He entered the small but bright front lobby, turning to look behind him out toward the street. No sign of being followed, but he expected they knew where he lived. He would grab a few things and lay low in his other apartment for a while – the apartment under another name. Roy had advised him years ago to establish a 'safe house' in case of emergency. Bruce assumed paranoia from his friend, but heeded the advice. Bruce preferred to call it his retreat. Either way, on this day he was glad for listening to his mentor.

But first things first. Mrs. Wilson's cat remained his responsibility for another day. It would take no more than two minutes to go to the apartment directly above his, dump a scoop of food in the cat's dish, and remove a scoop or two from the litter box. She'd asked Bruce to brush Bob daily, but he was certain Bob would survive one day without a grooming. Bruce wondered why a woman would name a cat after her dead spouse, especially when she always complained about what a lousy husband he'd been.

He opened the door to see Bob sitting in front of his dish, looking at him with a 'how dare you make me wait this long to eat' look. On the kitchen counter there lay a brightly coloured sticky note with a smiley face doodled below a neat 'Thanks Brucey!' He generously overfilled the dish, in part out of guilt for showing up late, and more for doubting he'd be back tomorrow to feed Bob before Mrs. Wilson returned late in the evening. Feeling bad for the lonely cat, he bent on one knee, rubbing behind the cat's ears as it ate. His mind drifted to Emmaline and her parting kiss. Snapping out of it, he realized he'd better get down to his place and toss a few essentials in a bag. As he stood up, he heard a loud noise from below.

"Shit," he said out loud without realizing it. He was sure the sound came from his apartment door getting kicked in. He'd have to buy some clothes tomorrow. He hurried quietly over to Mrs. Wilson's window, hoping to flee down the fire escape. He didn't want to alert those in his apartment below to his presence directly above them. There were a couple of masked goons milling around the bottom of the fire escape, fortunately not looking up as he looked out. He'd have to find another way out. He walked briskly to the front door and looked out the peephole. No sign of anyone. With care, he nudged opened the door, straining to see through the one inch crack that he created. He didn't see much, but heard voices.

"You two take the third floor. Knock on every door and find him. Knock them down if you have to. We know he's in here somewhere. The two of us will finish on this floor then head down to one. The front and back doors are covered. So is the fire escape. He's not going anywhere!"

Bruce slowly closed the door, hooked on the chain, and set the deadbolt. Frantic, he scanned the apartment. No way out. He'd have to find someplace to hide here. He went room to room looking. Nothing obvious jumped out at him. Not that he wanted obvious. He heard the tenants scream as the thugs broke down the door next to Mrs. Wilson's.

"Get out of the building! Now!" One of the men yelled at the tenants. "Call the police and you're dead – understand?"

"Maybe…" Bruce talked to himself as he continued his search. He went to the bedroom closet and moved her clothes aside. She lived on the top floor. He looked up and there it was; a door up to a crawlspace above the apartment. He put a stool in the closet and stepped up to boost himself into the very tight crawlspace. He reached back down, tugging at her hanging clothes until they covered most of the stool and concealed the door to the crawlspace. Then he waited.

In his mind's clock, he lay there forever, each second longer than the prior. The temperature was surely 40 degrees Celsius up there. He was dripping, trying not to breathe heavily. He lay and he listened. First, he heard a knocking at the apartment door, followed by a loud meow and a horrible hissing sound from Bob, trying to scare them off like a dog does with a bark. Bruce heard the door splinter as it busted inward.

"Take the bedroom and bathroom," he heard one of them shout to the other. He heard the one guy enter the bedroom and rip open the curtains. The man probably looked under the bed too. Then the moment of truth. He heard the man rustling through the clothes in the closet, just in case Bruce hid amongst them.

"Nothing in here," the voice moved away from the bedroom.

**137**

"He was here alright. There's a note on the kitchen counter and the cat's been fed recently. The boys would have got him if he went down the fire escape. Templeton's got to still be in the building somewhere. Let's go tell the boss."

Bruce heard the men leave, but he stayed sweating in the same position. He wanted to make sure they were gone, and might stay there all night if he had to. Maybe he'd sweat off those few pounds he'd struggled to lose. A few minutes slipped away before he heard what sounded like splashing water. It came from almost directly below him. The sound definitely came from within Mrs. Wilson's apartment, but didn't sound like it came from the bathroom. He wanted to look, but obviously someone had returned if they had turned on the water. He lay there, still, wondering what they were doing.

"Soak it good, but hurry up." Bruce could hear a man bellow below him.

Were they going to flood his apartment by having her water pour down into his? It certainly seemed odd. He would have his answer soon.

A violent swooshing sound burst the silence. But it wasn't water. It was the sound of a fire igniting. They'd poured gasoline or some other flammable liquid throughout the building and were torching it. Their prey was trapped and now they were finishing the kill.

*Now what, Bruce?* There was no going down the way he came. He could smell the smoke below him. He could touch the heat seeping through the ceiling. He looked around the crawl space. It spread out to cover the whole upper floor. Bruce began crawling like there was no tomorrow, as there might not be if he didn't figure out something soon.

**138**

He went to another opening that he figured must be a few apartments away. He couldn't see any smoke snaking through the cracks, and the beams were cooler to the touch. He flung open the door. Jumping down, Bruce came crashing hard through a rack of clothes onto the old hardwood floor. He crawled along the floor for a few feet, forgetting temporarily that he didn't need to any more. He rushed to the apartment's smashed door to assess the fire in the hallway and adjoining stairwell. They'd ransacked this unit too, and it smelled of gas. It just hadn't caught flame yet.

The hallway was bad. No sooner had he ducked his head out the door than he pulled it back in to escape a sudden surge in the flames. No clear path remained to the closest stairwell, which looked engulfed in flames anyway. The stairwell at the other end of the hall didn't look any better. There were flames hugging the walls on both sides.

Bruce turned to go back into the apartment he had just crashed through, but was interrupted by the sound of meowing. He turned back to the hallway to see Bob the cat sitting about twenty feet away, paralyzed by the flames.

"Shit!" A few years ago he would have just said screw the cat and run for safety. Instead, he made a run into danger. Keeping low and dodging the flames, Bruce darted down the hall and scooped up Bob. Greeted by an appreciative furry head rubbing against his chin, a flame erupting beside them triggered a frightened claw digging into his side. Stutter-stepping to avoid flare-ups, he traversed a similar path back to the apartment that either held his escape or would be his tomb. The living room walls were starting to burn, reducing the tacky wallpaper to

**139**

black ribbons. Darting through the entrance, the smoke thickened. Bruce fell to the floor to evade the smoke and began to crawl, Bob in tow. This unit was on the other side of the building, so he hoped the fire escape wasn't guarded. Even if it was, he thought a bullet to the head or getting beaten to death was better than burning alive.

The window to the fire escape was closed, not wanting to cooperate with Bruce's escape. He struggled a couple of times to open it, thinking at first that trying to open it with Bob in his left arm was the problem. Bruce pried the claws out of his shirt and sat him down briefly, hoping two hands would provide the necessary leverage. He had no better luck – and felt his leg turn into a scratching post by a seriously distressed feline. He picked up the squirming cat, which clawed at the window. Of course! The window was latched at the top – right where the cat swiped! Bruce never latched his window, so he didn't think to look for it. The flames were beginning to enter the bedroom, cutting off his route to anywhere but the fire escape, yet he still cautiously looked to the ground below. What he saw was a transport speeding away, no doubt the getaway vehicle for the thugs.

As he put one leg out the window, a loud bang sounded behind him, the bedroom door crashing in flames to the floor, the hinges released from the door frame's hold as the jamb burned away. Bruce didn't need any more prodding. Out he went onto the stoop, scurrying down the creaking, rusty metal stairs. Now he feared plummeting to his death when the fire escape gave way. As he rounded a corner on his descent, a flash of flames caused him to lurch backwards, momentarily cutting off his downward spiral. He continued, seeing the plume retreat to the confines of the building. Pushing free of the swaying ladder, he kept running for an entire block. He looked back down the hill to get a glimpse of his former home. It was completely engulfed in flames as firemen approached the scene. Bob finally let Bruce put him down. Bruce bent over, hands on knees, to catch his breath. He looked up from that position, forehead dripping in sweat. It was a spectacular blaze that was in danger of spreading to adjoining turn of the century buildings.

Bruce caught his breath for a few more seconds, then turned and walked hurriedly into the dark of the night. Bob followed. Bruce would have to disappear for a while.

Dale J. Moore

# 24 *The Bribe*

Peter and Deborah Lucas had received public ridicule on a number of broadcasts for forgetting their own son's age. As parents, they knew they were right of course. An appointment with Mr. Antonelli was exceptionally hard to come by, and the Lucases were stunned when they were granted one the same day they called. They fully expected to start with some third or fourth level lieutenant and have to work their way up to a meeting with Mr. Antonelli. Yet here they sat, trying to keep their agitation levels up, while admiring the rare artifacts that anointed his waiting room.

"This is like a museum in here." Peter admired a vase kept safely inside a protective enclosure flooded with light to show every hue of colour.

"Can you image his office?" Deborah stood admiring a painting on the wall.

"I guess it pays to own a health care monopoly."

"It certainly does…" There stood Mr. Antonelli. "I am so glad to meet you, Deborah and Peter." He stepped forward and gently shook both of their hands. "Please, let's go into my office."

Deborah led the way into the expansive space that served as Mr. Antonelli's home away from home. If they had known Mr. Antonelli, they would have known that he spent more time at this 'home' than his real home. Peter and Deborah were both surprised to see an extremely sparse office. It held no fantastic antiques like the waiting room. A few black and white photos hung scattered about the walls. A few doors concealed other rooms, except for one. Its door was ajar enough to see a dining area the size of a small restaurant.

"I am so pleased to meet the parents of one of our greatest scientists. You must be proud beyond words."

In unison, they both said "Yes, we are."

"All of us at UbiquiMed are confident that he will lead his team to cure all cancer within five years. Can you imagine? I never thought that I'd see the day!"

Deborah and Peter were still hung up on the first sentence. Specifically, the last two words 'five years.' The opulent surroundings and the pleasant greeting had silently ushered their hostility to the back of their minds, but that phrase awoke their slumbering anxiety.

"That's what we came here for, sir," Peter started.

"Our son should be free in two months," Deborah quickly followed, speaking louder than she intended.

"Free? What do you mean 'Free?'"

"From your program. He'll be twenty-five soon. That was the agreement. No doubt you've heard the rumours that he is only twenty-three."

The door from the dining room opened wider. Solomon Reynolds entered the room.

Peter's and Deborah's reasons to hate this man were many. Peter lost his cool at the sight of Reynolds. Turning red with rage, Peter took a few angry steps toward his tormentor as he spoke.

"You prick! I'm going to …"

A very large bodyguard emerged from the dining room, taking up position beside Reynolds. Peter stopped in his tracks.

With his protection in place, Solomon's tone was stern. "As I was going to say, all official records will confirm that your son is twenty-three."

"But …" Deborah tried to object.

Reynolds raised his hand to signal Deborah to stop talking. She did.

"Listen," he continued, "we both know the truth, but all the records will prove him to have two more years in the program. I think for the sake of humanity, we both know that he needs to continue his work in the program."

"We agree that he should continue his work. But he should be able to choose where he does it. Don't you think he deserves to start living his life?"

"He doesn't know any different. He's used to it. It might be bad for him to have to live on his own."

"That's for him to decide, not UbiquiMed."

Mr. Antonelli could see that what seemed logical to him and Reynolds, was not going to convince his star scientist's parents. He stood briefly with his hand on his chin, thinking. Methodically, he turned and walked over to his desk.

"Well, this discussion isn't going anywhere, I fear. Mr. Reynolds warned me it would go this way. I had my assistant prepare this envelope for you earlier, hopeful that I would be presenting it in a happier environment."

He handed Deborah the envelope. She opened it and pulled out a letter. A bank card fell out of the letter as she unfolded the paper. Peter bent down and picked it up. Her eyes moved back and forth as she read over it.

"Why don't you read it aloud, Mrs. Lucas?"

"To Peter and Deborah Lucas: It is with great honour and satisfaction that we present you with your first payment from the Orchid cure. It represents your percentage of one month's profit realized from its distribution." Her eyes went large, transfixed in disbelief on the printed figure. She handed the letter to Peter and stood there with her mouth partially agape. This cheque equalled what they made combined in a year, and these cheques were scheduled monthly.

Peter looked at it in amazement as well.

Mr. Antonelli spoke. "Well earned, I should say. And if you don't put up a fuss about this whole age nonsense, I will double your percentage on Orchid."

Deborah stood there with her hand on her hip. "Are you trying to buy our silence?"

Reynolds answered for Mr. Antonelli. His tone was condescending and his smile as fake as his concern. "Call it what you may, but you really have no alternative. No one would believe you and you would be publicly chastised. I don't think that we even needed to make this offer."

Mr. Antonelli added, "Besides, the boy knows nothing about 'getting out.' None of them do. They think that's just the way life is. So let them be. Let the world be a better place for the cures they develop."

"And what if we don't accept your bribe?"

Reynolds looked down at the ground for a few seconds. He then looked up, anger emitting from his eyes. His neck veins strained and facial muscles tensed with his firm reply.

"Do you think that, after paying for his education, his housing, his food for twenty plus years, not to mention a small fortune in state-of- the-art medical research equipment, we are simply going to let him walk out the door and take all of his knowledge to a competitor? Over someone's dead body! And it won't be mine!"

Dale J. Moore

# 25 *Simple Plan*

The layout of the UbiquiMed complex wasn't that complicated, but had a few perplexing items. Justin did the best he could to memorize every hallway, turn, and possible exit. He'd never thought of himself as a prisoner, but he was now certain that he would have to 'escape' from this complex to help his parents. Only one day had passed since the news report about their kidnapping, but it was a long 24 hours of planning and worrying.

He completed his analysis of the electrical systems information that he stumbled upon during his frequent, but brief forays into the main system computer. As he stood in the sonic shower, all of the components of his plan raced through his head. He felt somewhat unsure of his plan, as he had no idea what lay outside his home's walls except for what he'd seen in those layouts. Much like his work, he tried to anticipate all possible scenarios. Unlike his work, he had limited information. Unlike his work, he couldn't run multiple simulations until he got it right. He'd settled on invoking his plan at 11:30 in the morning, that being the standard lunch break time.

Justin went about his morning as usual. He submitted some new tests for execution today before beginning his examination of yesterday afternoon's results. Where he was in the process, he could do in his sleep. And that was good; his mind wasn't on his work. His mind fixated on details and what-if scenarios.

The plan was simple. He would find Chantelle and Nagesh. Justin felt sure that he could get them to go with him. They would make their way to the exit at the south end of the mountain. It appeared that there might be a quicker exit to the north, but it looked like it came out directly in front of the main entrance. He hoped to avoid detection and the south entrance looked like it came out on the backside of the mountain, away from the busy corridors and likely heavy security at the main entrance. He'd packed a bag with some extra clothes, although all standard issue UbiquiMed lab uniforms. He wasn't sure how he would get new clothes, nor how he would acquire any money. But he was determined to get away from the UbiquiMed lies and deception that were beginning to pile up the size of the mountain on which the complex was built.

He'd sent a few cryptic messages to Chantelle and Nagesh, but wasn't certain if they knew what he was planning. Justin had a sense that Chantelle had an inkling as her responses were equally cryptic. The lunch time reminder popped up on his FID, breaking his concentration.

Time to start.

With speed, he navigated a memorized path to the electrical grid system. He found quite easily how to shut the power down. The trick was how to shut down the emergency backup system. All the emergency exits stayed locked without both systems coming down – meaning the door to the corridor remained locked as it had almost the entire time he lived there. Not a single person had stepped foot in his home for at least the past ten years.

Justin figured that shutting down both systems should give him ten minutes to get to the south exit. Based on the distance and the perceived steepness of the exit stairs, he would have less than five minutes to find and persuade Chantelle and Nagesh to go with him. He looked outside to see a perfectly sunny day. He counted on the sunlight to provide some lighting to his escape.

Everything was set up. One simple command and all the power should be shut down. Justin typed the command. He sat quietly, fixated on his FID, not yet executing the command. He grabbed his supplies bag, took a deep breath, and firmly said "Execute."

Everything went dark.

He held out his hand and could barely make out its outline. Why was it so dark? He looked out the window – the sun was gone too. Like a visually impaired person put in new surroundings, Justin took care to navigate to his balcony window. He couldn't believe his eyes as he got closer. There was no outside. Only inside. Not only had the sun disappeared, but so had the sky, the trees, and even the entire mountain. Through the darkness, he could make out the barren inside of a very large building. Even where he lived was a lie! The scenery that he'd enjoyed for years was assuredly an elaborate hologram or artificial environment of some sort. He stood stunned, staring into the emptiness in front of him for a few seconds, before remembering the clock was ticking. A minute wasted, and everything would surely take longer in the pitch black of night that he'd created. For all Justin knew, maybe it was night time in the real world. Hopefully he'd find out for sure in about eight and a half minutes.

The door to the corridor sprang open in response to the power outage, as he saw on a schematic. There were a few whispers of light slipping innocently through the doorway into his home, the source being a battery powered exit sign in the never seen before hallway. He edged his head out into the corridor, looking both left and right. A few heads were sticking out of doors to the left, much like his own, but no one had ventured out into the hallway. He stepped out then turned right. From seeing Chantelle exercising in her sunroom, and from looking at the layout, he believed her to live in the second unit down from this. He also assumed Nagesh lived between them. Backpack bouncing as he ran down the hall, Justin called their names.

About twenty metres ahead of him, Chantelle stepped out into the hallway. As he closed the gap to her, Nagesh came out behind him and spoke.

"Justin0727! What are you doing?"

Justin ran a few more steps before reaching for Chantelle's hand. She gave it to him, the sensation temporarily overwhelming Justin. He hadn't touched another person for as long as he could remember, and had longed for the day to hold *her* hand. He looked in her eyes and she returned the stare. Her smile warmed him all over. He wanted to just stand there in that moment and enjoy the sensation, but he had other things to focus on.

Chantelle looked at Justin and asked, "Yes, what are we -- I mean you -- doing?" She did not look concerned like Nagesh.

"I'm getting out of here." Justin continued to hold fast onto Chantelle's hand as he pulled her along, half-running to where Nagesh stood.

"But why?" Nagesh asked.

"The lies," Chantelle answered for Justin.

Elated, Justin said, "So I'm not the only one that sees it! What a relief."

Tentative, Nagesh weighed his decision. "They treat us well here. The outside world is …"

Justin completed the sentence. "Is fake, is what it is. Did you look outside after I shut the power down?"

"You shut the power down? How'd you do that?" Nagesh asked

"Later. Did you look outside?" Justin replied, looking at his watch, anxious to get moving.

"Yes. It disappeared," Nagesh responded.

"I figure we've got just over six minutes to get out of here. So if you're in, follow me. If not, it's been a pleasure working with you."

Justin looked intently at Nagesh. Chantelle's grip had never loosened so Justin knew her position. She was going.

Sensing Justin's urgency, Nagesh quickly answered.

"All right. I trust you Justin0727. Let's go."

"Back this way." Justin led them back down the hallway past his unit. A few people were now standing partially in the hallway, looking at the three of them running toward them.

"We're leaving, if you want to come with us," Justin yelled as he ran.

Most of the people were scared and ducked quickly back into their units. One young lady recognized Justin from the press broadcasts and stepped firmly out into the hallway. When they got even with her, she fell in line behind them and started to run also. As they approached the next door down, the new girl shouted ahead.

"George1608 … come on! Let's get out of here."

George1608 looked at her. Kiara2407 was his team lead. So he followed.

The next doorway contained a female team member of theirs. She heard the commotion but stayed in the doorway.

"I'm sorry. I just can't!" The young woman stepped back into the darkness of her unit.

The group continued to run, following Justin's obviously planned turns. He lit up his watch to look at the time. It would be close. They turned another corner and came upon a long upward stretch of stairs.

"This is a long hike up. We have to hurry, but you can't burn yourself out in the first minute. So let's keep a steady pace. At the top is a door out of the complex. Then we are free. But we need to get there in three minutes."

The stairs were unending in the darkness. They pressed forward. Fortunately, UbiquiMed had them all on a daily exercise routine, so Justin figured they all should be in decent shape. He lit up his watch again.

"How much time?" George1608 panted as he asked. He wished now that he'd actually run on the treadmill a few times when he let it spin on its own to avoid working out. He'd never imagined the need to run anywhere.

"Just over a minute left. We should be seeing the door soon," Justin replied.

"Let's hope so." George1608 hesitated for a second to catch his breath. "I'd hate to go all this way for nothing."

"Shouldn't we be seeing some light by now?" Kiara2407 asked.

Justin glanced back at her, while still jogging up the stairs. He collided with something, falling hard backward and knocking down Chantelle with him.

"I think you found the door," Kiara2407 laughed.

"Quick, open it!" Justin yelled as he lay holding his shoulder.

George1608 stepped forward, pushed it open, and stepped through. Justin followed and held the door as the others rushed out to the open air and blue sky. Nagesh was the last one through their escape outlet. The instant he came through the door, Justin started to close it. Swinging the door closed, the lighting in the stairwell came on, signaling the restoration of power to the facility. The group listened for an alarm, but none was heard.

"We must have got out just in time," George1608 said, bent over sucking air.

"Let's hope it takes them a little while to realize we're gone," Justin said, as they all began to look around. They exited from a small building, and were surprised to find themselves standing on relatively flat ground, not the side of a mountain. Their eyes took a few moments to adjust to the bright sunlight. As they looked around, they saw a city a few scant blocks away. They were in the middle of a park! People casually strolled on a nearby sidewalk. Others rode serenely by on their bicycles. Joggers talked to each other as they ran past.

"This doesn't look like the violent, war torn place that we've been told about, now does it?" Chantelle remarked.

"I knew it!" Kiara shouted as she jumped up and down. "I could tell from the news conference. The background was all wrong. I've searched to uncover the truth since then."

"Me too!" Justin grabbed her hands and held them. "I knew something was wrong. I got outside the UbiquiMed network and started to uncover their lies."

Put off a little by Justin grabbing this other girl's hands, Chantelle walked around the corner of the building, partly in silent protest, and also to see more of their new world.

"Guys … you should come here," she called out.

They all came around the building. Not only were they not on a mountain, but before them lay a huge bay of water, with a small island about a kilometre or so off shore. It had a bright UbiquiMed sign on it. They continued their panoramic view, turning to see an expansive orange bridge magnificently span the opening to the sea.

"The Golden Gate Bridge," Nagesh informed the others, like they didn't know. They'd all seen it in their learning while growing up. The last they heard though, it had a gaping hole in it from an explosion. Obviously repaired, many years may have passed since the incident for all they knew.

"Were we under water this whole time?" George questioned, also apparently stating the obvious. "The entire world that we knew was a lie, wasn't it?"

Justin replied, "I'm afraid so. But we can't dwell on it for now. We've got to get away from here. Let's follow the water into the city."

Dale J. Moore

# 26 *Breaking News*

The morning writing session of 'Such is Life' was eerily quiet, a stark contrast to most mornings, when voices challenged each other to be heard at times. Gone was the boisterous role playing and ensuing outbursts of unimpeded laughter. Even the breakfast bagels lay on their tray, victims of a collective loss of appetite. An empty chair at the end of the table loomed large in everyone's minds. The team sat around the expansive conference table, note pads and pens lying unspent in front of them. The pads had leftover ideas from the previous day doodled chaotically across them, but no new ideas had found ink to lay on paper.

At one end of the conference room a large FID displayed the news. The morning news was one of the biggest sources for their parodies and sarcasm. They often flipped through stations, but the American Network remained their favourite. That particular network's extremely serious manner was perfect fodder for the 'Such is Life' writers. Bruce's constipated impersonation of the anchor was a regular bit on the show.

Today, the 'Such is Life' team watched in disbelief at the lead story on all the networks.

"A horrific fire broke out in San Francisco last night, claiming the life of comedian Bruce Templeton," the announcer started, as footage of a fire raged in the background. "The entire apartment building was engulfed in flames in a matter of minutes. Mr. Templeton is most recently known as the host of 'Such is Life', a news parody show based in San Francisco. He was forty-six years old and single. He is survived by a sister and brother. The cause of the fire is not yet known."

"Not yet known, my ass," Tulio blurted out. "A fire like that isn't from someone dropping a match accidentally. I know that Antonelli and UbiquiMed were behind this."

"Tulio, you should watch what you say," Ingrid half-whispered to him, appearing afraid someone was watching or listening.

"He told me some of UbiquiMed's goons roughed him up the other day."

"Maybe we should have held back a bit on those UbiquiMed stories."

"Bruce wasn't about to be intimidated. He still believed in journalistic freedom, even if it is still partially regulated."

"And look where it got him."

Everyone else in the room remained silent.

"I think we should just show a rerun today and go home." Tulio stood up as he made his statement.

"Maybe the team can put together a 'best of' tribute and run that today."

"Good idea." Tulio sat back down again. "Remember that skit last year when he imitated the First Gentleman dancing?"

The room started to get loud with everyone laughing as they recalled the skit.

"And the one where he dressed up like the President playing poker with the Joint Chiefs of Staff?"

The whole room buzzed with voices blurting out various sketches from the sometimes-twisted brain of Bruce. Others reminisced of sketches he starred in, and the laughable characters he created for the camera.

"We might have to stretch this out for a couple of days!" Tulio wiped tears from his eyes, laughing so hard.

"So this is what an Irish wake is like!" Ingrid exclaimed.

"So where's the booze?" Tulio asked, extending an empty glass.

Dale J. Moore

# 27 *Hideout*

The night before replayed in Bruce's mind over and over in an endless loop. The same scenes rolled a thousand times over. Hiding. Laying still. Not breathing. Listening. Crawling. Dodging flames. Clambering down the fire escape. Watching his former home fade from existence in a blaze that disrupted the night sky with its brilliance. It was disturbing to see repeatedly with no ability to control or even slow down the images. His hands shook, recalling his thoughts intrinsically anchored to each series of images. His life never flashed in front of his eyes, but at different points in the night Bruce convinced himself he'd never see Emmaline again. And now he couldn't see her, at least without risking her life. He wasn't willing to take that chance, no matter how much it hurt knowing she thought him dead. *Was it wrong to hope that she mourn his passing?* He was sure UbiquiMed thought him dead, and Bruce needed them to keep thinking that. The goons had seen him go in and they had all the exits covered as it burned to the ground. Surely they'd assume he'd died. Tragically, horribly burned remains were found at the scene. There wasn't much left to identify the victims. Bruce knew it would be weeks before they were identified. Sometimes in blazes like this one, identification had to be assumed rather than confirmed.

The apartment in which Bruce hid out was known only to him. It was his safe house. He hadn't even brought a woman friend here. One night he got pretty close to breaking his rule, but managed to use his celebrity to get a room in a fully booked hotel.

He flipped on the morning news and thought of the crew at the office sitting around the conference table writing the gags for today's show. He was startled and unnerved to see his own face in the upper corner of the screen, with a fire blazing in the background. He laughed for a moment, realizing the footage wasn't even from his apartment. He then thought about what Emmaline must be thinking. Certain that she cared for him as much as he did for her, he wanted to let her know that he was okay but didn't risk it. For now, he'd have to play dead.

The location of his hideout was chosen for its proximity to his work. He hadn't chosen it for standing in the shadows of the UbiquiMed West Coast headquarters, the same building where Mr. Antonelli had the top floor as his private penthouse. The proximity was a bad coincidence. Bruce would be extra careful with coming and going to avoid recognition by someone from UbiquiMed.

For now, he had a few weeks' worth of food and no plan. For now, he wasn't even sure that he even wanted revenge. For now, he just wished he had Emmaline trapped in his hideout with him.

# 28 *Fresh Air*

The escapees walked briskly down the waterfront, trying to put some distance between them and the building which served as their portal to freedom. The walk turned into a light jog. Following the waterfront towards what looked like the downtown area seemed like the right course of action. Their eyes roamed as they went, taking in the beauty of the new world around them. A multitude of new sights blessed their eyes. The air smelled different. It tasted different. Their eyes were still adjusting to real sunlight, from the manmade light of their lifetime homes.

"I'd rather be walking leisurely and soaking up the sun," Kiara proclaimed, jogging beside Nagesh.

"Wouldn't we all!" George replied, as yet not recovered from the stair climb.

"We need to get out of these uniforms," was the matter-of-fact response from Justin.

"Yeah we stick out, that's for sure," Chantelle replied, inspecting the group. "We look like convicts that broke out of prison."

"Didn't we?" asked Kiara.

"I've got some money but don't know what it will buy us." Justin had some old money that he'd kept in a small box, along with a very old picture of his parents. He just hoped the money still held some value.

"Hey …" a jogger called out to them from the other side of the road. "Say, aren't you Justin Lucas, the famous scientist?"

They were all stunned as the man walked closer. Chantelle looked at Justin and mouthed 'Justin Lucas'?

"Yeah, it is you."

Nobody in the group had said a word as the man looked over the rest of them.

"And you two … you're his team, aren't you? I'm sorry, but I'm blanking out on your names."

"Chantelle0206."

"Nagesh1410."

The man looked at them strangely as they stated their names. He shrugged and continued. Walking up to Justin, he surrounded the young scientist with a bear-like embrace.

For someone who hadn't even touched a person in many years, a hug from a complete stranger was a surprising experience. Justin looked at the others and shook his head to show he didn't know what was going on.

"You cured my Dad, man. You saved his life." The man went over and hugged Nagesh for a second. He then proceeded over to Chantelle and wrapped her up in his arms. He was apparently enjoying this one more than the other hugs.

"You're welcome," Justin said, agitated by the prolonged embrace with Chantelle. "We were just doing our jobs."

"And modest too. How can I ever repay you?"

"Well, we could use some clothes."

The jogger reached into his front pocket and pulled out some money. "Sorry, but I don't carry much on me when I run … just some in case of an emergency … my wife's idea to carry any at all actually. But you can have it." He reached forward with the money.

Chantelle grabbed it out of his hand, smiled and said "Thank you."

"What's with the uniforms anyway? Did you guys forget to change before leaving the lab for the day?"

"It's a long story. We'll pay you back. What's your name?" Justin asked.

"Don't worry about it. My treat. Sorry I didn't have more. Good luck." The jogger patted Justin on the shoulder, turned, and resumed his run.

Grateful for the money, they continued on their way, cutting across a park and past Fort Mason. George was happy with this course, as it circumnavigated a large hill. The last thing he needed was another hill. As they passed, he noticed that the buildings looked much too old for structures built during or since the Dark Years. Passing the fort, the orange-clad group turned back to the waterfront, walking down Beach Street.

Navigating traffic for the first time ever in their lives, they eventually made it across the street to the larger walkway nearer the water. Nagesh and Chantelle walked together, as did George and Kiara.

They all continued to soak up their new surroundings. There were a lot of couples walking hand in hand, so George suggested to Kiara that they do the same. Kiara was a little unsure, but agreed to do so. Human touch was new to all of them and didn't come easy. The softness of Kiara's hand felt good to George, but she was uncomfortably holding on.

Nagesh and Chantelle stopped for a minute to watch and listen to a man standing in a gazebo playing guitar and singing, as well as playing the harmonica on occasion between lyrics. A small crowd was gathered around as they mingled while waiting near the streetcar turnaround. Justin stood a row or so back and watched, although he spent much of the time looking at Chantelle, enjoying her smile and her fine black hair swaying gently with the breeze off the water.

George and Kiara stopped a little bit ahead, hands no longer attached, as they waited for the others to catch up. Since they didn't know their destination, they didn't want to get too far ahead and lose the others. Face to face was their only means of communication – no pop-up FID to summon someone.

The musician finished his song and nodded toward his open guitar case, looking for a reward for his effort. Nagesh watched in awe as people stepped up and tossed money in the case. Chantelle started to walk away, noticing Kiara waiting for them across the intersection. Chantelle had gone six or seven steps when she noticed Nagesh wasn't by her side. Slowing her pace toward Kiara, she looked back over her shoulder to find Nagesh. Suddenly, Justin grabbed Chantelle by the arm, pulling her violently towards him, causing her to land awkwardly on top of him as they tumbled to the ground. She looked in his eyes briefly before her eyes jerked to the side at the sound of an old-fashioned streetcar clicking by. She screamed into his face as it rattled by within a metre of their heads. She'd had no idea the streetcar was coming and it certainly would have killed her if Justin hadn't grabbed her.

People stood by clapping at the heroic effort.

A man bent over and extended his hand to Justin to help him off the ground. "Say, aren't you Justin Lucas?"

"Yes, I am. Thank you."

"Look everyone, it's Justin Lucas. The guy's not busy enough saving people from cancer, he's got to save them from streetcars too!"

Attention was the last thing that Justin or the others wanted. He put up a hand to say thanks before scurrying across the street to get away from the gathered crowd. The other escapees soon followed, catching up to him a block later.

Chantelle was first to catch up, tugging at him from behind.

"Thanks for saving me," and she gave him a hug. A real hug. Not a nice-to-see-you hug. He felt the warmth of her body up against his and started to blush as the others approached.

Nagesh spoke as the others caught up.

"That was something, Justin! I hollered when I saw the streetcar coming, but it would have been too late if you weren't there!"

"Yes, but so much for being inconspicuous and blending in," Justin responded.

"The Wharf," Kiara read the colourful sign with the crab that lay ahead. "Looks busy – and interesting."

"Sorry, no time for sightseeing right now. I see some little shops across the street. Let's see what this money will buy us." Justin half-pointed in the direction of the small souvenir shops that dotted the street.

The five merged into the crowd of people crossing the street, separating a bit so as not to look like a sea of uniforms. They still got a few stares. The storefront was busy with racks of t-shirts and sweatshirts, with large SALE signs plastered on top of each rack.

Justin looked at the prices, realizing how little he could buy with the money he had. "Let's see if there's anything cheaper inside the store."

They looked around, flipping up sleeves for price tags to confirm the prices. The group had spread throughout the store looking for a bargain.

"Hey! Over here!" Kiara summoned them over. "Here's the cheapest rack in the store."

The rack had a varied selection of remnants, no two items looking the same. Most had the words 'San Francisco' emblazoned across the chest.

"It certainly is an amazing array of colours!" Nagesh said, holding up a bright orange sweatshirt.

"The idea is not to stick out, remember? They could spot you in the dark if you wore that!" Chantelle laughed at her own remark. The others joined her in a good laugh as Nagesh held it up against himself and looked in a nearby mirror.

"Look," Justin said, counting his money for the third time, "we've only got enough for two of these shirts."

"So who gets them?" asked George.

"The girls should get them," Nagesh replied. "As much as I like this orange shirt, I think the girls should get them. They will be safer if they can blend in."

Justin nodded agreement.

"Good thinking, Nagesh. All agreed?"

Everyone nodded. The girls each grabbed a sweatshirt and gave them to Justin to pay.

"We have souvenir pens on sale today, would you like one?"

"Oh, no thanks. Just the shirts please." Justin didn't even have enough change left to buy a pen.

"Is there someplace we can change into these?" Kiara had come up to the counter behind Justin and grabbed the bag after he paid the cashier.

"In the back, on the left."

"Thanks." Kiara and Chantelle headed off to the change room, emerging moments later sporting their new sweatshirts.

"You should have gone with the orange," Nagesh kidded Chantelle as she walked by.

"What do you want us to do with the uniform tops?" Chantelle held them up to Justin. Walking out of the store, Justin took the bag from her and deposited it in a nearby trash can.

"Where to?" George asked.

"Let's keep along the waterfront. Lots of people to blend in with. You guys stay in two's again, one guy and one girl, but stay a little bit further apart. I'll follow a few metres behind. I want to separate the uniforms. Let's just walk so we don't draw attention – we aren't dressed like joggers."

The twenty minute walk along the waterfront was very relaxing for everyone. In spite of constantly looking around in a paranoid fashion, even Justin was able to calm down slightly. At least the heartbeat settled to a normal rate. The spectacle of the waterfront views was soon replaced by the stunning panoramas of the downtown buildings on the opposite side of the roadway. Some were ancient looking structures and others were gleaming, towering feats of architecture.

Justin broke the tranquility of the stroll. "We need to head away from the water and into the downtown."

George looked away from the water to the downtown. "Hills. Great."

Sensing his desire to stop and not go any further, Kiara reached over and grabbed his hand.

"Come on, George1608. Let's go see the rest of San Francisco!"

# **29** *Directions*

Coolness crept into the air as the early evening sun began to slip behind the hills of San Francisco. The short sleeve uniforms that the men still wore became insufficient against the slight chilling wind. George felt it the most, a direct result of his poor conditioning and the sweat cooling on his body. Their trip away from the water had achieved its desired result. They passed people on the sidewalk but much more sporadically than along the pier. Most importantly, they were going unnoticed, aside from the odd look at the uniforms.

"Where are we headed, besides up the hill?" Nagesh asked.

Justin stopped to answer, noticing George looked a little worse for wear and deciding a short break might help their slowest member catch his breath.

"I'm looking for my parents."

"Where do they live?" Chantelle asked.

"Doesn't matter. They've been kidnapped."

"How do you know?" she followed up.

"I saw it on a broadcast."

"What do you mean?" George asked, now standing up straight after recovering a bit.

**173**

"I was able to get outside the UbiquiMed firewall to this outside news program called 'Such is Life'."

"How'd you do that?" Nagesh was as puzzled as George.

"Likely the same way I did," interrupted Kiara.

Everyone turned to look at the youngest member of the group.

"I only got outside the network a few days ago. I'd been trying since the Orchid broadcast. Something about that didn't seem right, so I got curious."

Justin looked at her with surprise. She had taken the words right out his mouth.

"That's exactly what I thought. But I got a congratulatory note from someone that pointed me to the 'Such is Life' broadcast site. So I had an idea of where to go looking."

Kiara nodded her head in appreciation. "Yeah, I had trouble getting anywhere until yesterday. I got to a broadcast of some senate hearing in Washington. Pretty dry stuff. And I didn't have much time, with the logging UbiquiMed has in place."

Justin now looked at her in admiration. He thought himself pretty clever, devising a way around the UbiquiMed protocols, so now felt the same about this new girl.

"Alright, so you're both brilliant. We knew that before," George stated, jealous of the new bond between Justin and Kiara.

"George1608 is right. Where does that leave us with finding your kidnapped parents?" Chantelle replied, also somewhat bothered by the attention Justin was paying to Kiara.

Justin turned away from Kiara to face Chantelle.

"I'm fairly certain 'Such is Life' broadcasts from here in San Francisco. I was hoping to get out of the uniforms and ask around where their broadcast centre is located."

"So let me, or me and Kiara, ask around. We don't stick out quite as much as you guys."

"Good idea, Chantelle. We look like tourists," as Kiara stretched out her sweatshirt to prominently display the name 'San Francisco' that covered much of the front.

"Okay. Let's keep heading up this street. We'll drop back about ten metres so we don't look like we're with you."

"Oh yeah, we'll look great all together in our uniforms," George quipped.

"We can split up too," Nagesh answered. "I'll go on the other side of the street from you and Justin. We can all watch for the girls to signal us when they get the information from someone."

"Agreed. Good luck, girls," Justin replied.

They broke into three groups, as the girls trod up the street, away from Justin and George who stayed put for a minute to get some separation. Nagesh jogged across the street and walked slowly up the other sidewalk.

The guys watched the girls approach a lady to ask her, but the lady just ignored them and kept walking.

The next passersby were a couple of men, one with his arm around the shoulder of the other. Justin was too far back to hear the conversation, but saw some head shaking and shoulder shrugging that was an obvious no.

Chantelle and Kiara looked back at the guys for a moment and also shook their heads no, before moving on.

A young man and woman came around the corner and stopped at the girls' request.

"Do you know where the 'Such is Life' studio is?" Chantelle asked, hoping she'd have better luck than Kiara did with the last couple.

The man looked at them and replied. "Oh, no. We're just tourists from Seattle."

"Yes, see …" the young woman smiled and unzipped her jacket to show the same sweatshirt that Kiara was wearing. Kiara acknowledged the match.

"If you're looking for a good restaurant, we just had dinner at the small place around the corner. It was excellent." The man decided to pass on their find to their fellow tourists.

"And inexpensive too," the young woman added.

"Thanks for the tip," Chantelle replied, thinking that food did sound like a good idea. If only they had some way to pay for it. As the couple walked away, she looked across the street to Nagesh, giving him a thumbs-down sign.

The next ten or so people they passed all were wearing sweatshirts or jackets with San Francisco across the front or at least large SF letters on one side of the chest. They skipped asking any more tourist types. The street opened up ahead of them into a plaza area called Union Square. A man stood on the corner, his cap-covered head looking down at a paper.

"Excuse me, sir," Kiara politely began her question, "can you tell us where to find the 'Such is Life' building?"

The man looked up at them through sunglasses, surprised by the question and noticing their unusual ensemble of tourist shirt and medical pants. Likely just comfortable pants they picked up at some thrift store, he thought. Who knows, maybe it was a new trend the kids were into these days.

"You mean SF-NET?"

"Is that where they broadcast 'Such is Life'?"

"Yes it is. Why do a couple of tourists like you want to see that place? I mean, there are so many other attractions in this city. Like Union Square. You know they've got live entertainment starting soon."

"We need to ask some questions," Kiara replied, sounding like she was going to interrogate someone.

The man stood up straighter and folded his paper. Sensing his uneasiness about Kiara's response, Chantelle lightened the dialogue.

"Yes, we need to ask someone questions about working there. We want to get into broadcasting."

The man relaxed again. "It's just up on the right. Kitty corner to Union Square." He pointed to a yellow glass building that looked out of place from the older but immaculately kept neighbouring buildings.

"Thank you, sir," Kiara politely responded.

"Be careful in there, they can be ruthless I hear," the man warned them, lifting up his sunglasses to look straight into Chantelle's eyes, before bowing his head and ducking around the corner and into the crowd forming in the square.

Chantelle thought the comment was odd, but was just grateful he'd pointed out the place to them. They would have walked right by it on their own, looking for 'Such is Life' instead of SF-NET.

The girls motioned to Nagesh across the street, then collected Justin and George with a similar gesture. As they assembled as a group again, Chantelle filled them in, mentioning the curious exchange with the man who gave them directions to SF-NET.

In the past few minutes, the Square's population had swelled quickly. People flooded out of a nearby underground transport station and amassed in front of a stage with a huge video display behind it.

"Look at the size of that screen!"

No sooner were the words out of George's mouth, than the screen lit up brightly and flashed a series of UbiquiMed logos. An attractive young woman paraded out onto the stage from behind some scenery at the right.

"Hello San Francisco!" She paused for a few seconds to let some polite applause fade. "How's everyone doing tonight? What a great evening for Shakespeare! I'm very pleased to host tonight's performance by the San Francisco Repertory Company as they present King Lear. Before we start tonight's performance, please turn your attention to the video screen behind me, for a word from UbiquiMed, the people who made this free performance possible. Thank you, and enjoy the show!" She put her hands above her head, clapping a few times before slowly exiting to the opposite side from which she entered.

The humungous video screen filled completely with the UbiquiMed logo, an icon the team had seen every day of their lives, since age three. It was as familiar to them as their face in the mirror.

"I see that logo in my sleep some nights," Justin commented.

"I think it's burned into my retinas," laughed Chantelle.

The next image that appeared caught them all off guard. There in front of them was a twenty metre-high picture of Justin, Chantelle, and Nagesh standing together, with a flowering orchid logo glowing in the upper corner.

"Nice picture," Nagesh remarked, "too bad I never actually met you two face to face until today!"

"Just because we never sat in the same room doesn't mean we weren't a team!" Chantelle protested.

"Still, human contact would have been nice ..." he replied.

"You guys are celebrities!" George enthusiastically stated.

"No wonder people recognize you, Justin. Your name must be synonymous with the Orchid cure by now." Chantelle said, looking at her team leader.

"But you guys deserve as much credit as me," he humbly replied.

"It's always the leader that gets the credit ... or the blame. Just as well, I don't think I could stand all the attention," Nagesh laughed as he finished.

"Don't kid yourself, Nagesh. My picture may be twenty metres high, but yours is at least fifteen. Anyway, I don't think we should be standing around admiring our pictures. Somebody's going to recognize one of us."

"Yes, like me," said the man who had given the girls directions moments earlier. "What are you guys doing away from UbiquiMed? I didn't think they let you guys out into the general population."

"We ..." George started, but felt Justin's hand on his chest to stop him.

"What do you mean, sir?" Justin asked.

"I mean, I thought you guys were locked up in solitude until you were 25 years old. Isn't that the deal?"

The group looked at each other. None of them had heard of this arrangement and were perplexed by the statement. Before the conversation could continue, the advertisement ended on the huge screen.

"Urgent notice from the SFPD." A man sitting in an official looking office began to speak. "Five researchers from a UbiquiMed laboratory have gone missing after a chemical spill at their facility. They are possibly infected with a contagion and need to be brought back to UbiquiMed for immediate medical attention. Please avoid physical contact as you risk exposure, but notify the SFPD immediately if you spot them. They are wearing UbiquiMed uniforms and likely travelling together. There are three men and two women, all in their early twenties. Again, please do not hesitate to contact the SFPD, or our emergency number 999-UBIQUIMED. Thank you for helping us help these dedicated researchers."

A few people in the crowd looked at the five of them, and as fingers pointed at them, the rest of the crowd spread away in a circular pattern, much like grease when a drop of detergent is placed in water. Justin could see members of the crowd reaching for their transmitters, contacting the UbiquiMed hotline.

"Time to go, kids," the man called out to them.

"Why should we go with you?" Kiara asked.

"Because you don't want to be back at UbiquiMed in an hour. At least I'm guessing you are out for a reason."

"He's right," Justin agreed. "Let's go," he urged the man.

"Okay, follow me. We're going to cut through a few alleys and buildings to get away from here quickly. Then we'll figure out our next steps."

The man turned, heading down an alley filled with small restaurants. The five scientists followed closely behind, with Justin at the back of the group.

After a few twists and turns, detouring through a crowded restaurant, they surfaced in an empty alley, surrounded by trash bins.

"Okay, let's stop here for a minute," the man said, holding up his hand to the group.

"Thank God!" George panted.

"You've likely got transmitters implanted in you someplace. I'm not sure why they aren't tracking you just using those."

"I killed the power to the entire complex so we could escape. Maybe they're still recovering their systems."

"Let's hope so. That will buy us some time. How current are your location transmitters?"

The group looked around at each other.

"I don't think any of us knew we had them," Chantelle answered for them.

"Have you received any medical shots recently?"

Again, the group looked around. They all shook their heads no.

"I don't recall one in the past ten years … how about you guys?" Justin posed the question to the group. Again, a bunch of head shaking.

"Good. That likely means that you've got old tracking devices. The old ones aren't as precise as the new ones. The new ones can nail your location to within a few centimetres. The old ones you have are about a city block range. Much better for avoiding detection."

The constant worrier George expressed his concern again.

"Great. But how long can we run? It sounds like they'd still find us pretty quick."

"If we can keep you guys hidden for about fifteen minutes, I can get back to my apartment and get a descrambler for your tracking devices. It will effectively fry them."

"Why do you have a descrambling device in the first place?" Chantelle asked, concerned that he might not be the kind of new friend they wanted.

"I'll be glad to explain once we get your trackers disabled, and I get you back to my apartment. For now, we're going to have to do some more cutting through buildings and restaurants. No doubt they are beginning to close in on us as we stand here talking."

Chantelle and Kiara looked at Justin. He nodded his approval.

"Good. Follow me again. We'll get to another alley in about five minutes, at which time I'll leave you and double back to my apartment for the descrambler. I don't want to take you there directly, because UbiquiMed will go door to door in whatever neighbourhood your signal goes dead. Let's go."

And off they went, following him as before, once again with Justin at the tail of the procession.

It didn't seem long until they reached the next alley, but they must have covered more than five city blocks. The man got them safely to the alley, then bid his adieu and took off as promised.

"What do you think of this guy?" Nagesh queried.

"Good Samaritan type, I suppose," George responded.

"I'm sure there's more to it than that," Kiara contributed to the discussion, then looked at Justin. "What's the matter, Justin?"

"Not sure. There's something about that guy. Does he look familiar to any of you?"

"No". "No". "No, should he?" the chorus rang out.

"Not sure. But I feel that we can trust him and I'm not sure why."

The group looked around. Pretty clean for an alley. The garbage pails sat neatly in their designated areas by the back doors.

"So," Chantelle started to Kiara, trying to divert attention from Justin, "How long have you and George worked as a team?"

"Oh, about eighteen months, maybe. Does that sound about right, George?"

"Nineteen months and four days. If you're counting," he replied before moving over to where the guys were standing.

Kiara looked at him walking away, thinking it odd his answer so precise, but then again George was a very detailed and thorough researcher. Perhaps it spilled over into his personal life. Then she thought 'what personal life?' They got up, ate, worked, ate, worked some more, ate some more, slept, and repeated. Every day. No days off.

"So you guys must be pretty close, eh?" Chantelle prodded some more.

"I suppose. Since you mention it, I probably spend four hours a day talking to George."

"Yeah, same here. I mean same amount of time with Justin every day." Chantelle said, staking her claim.

"George is like a brother to me."

Chantelle looked at George. "Maybe so, but I don't think he sees you like a sister. Don't you notice how he looks at you?"

"You mean like the way you hang on every word Justin says?"

Chantelle was speechless. *Was she that obvious?*

"Don't worry, Chantelle. I think Justin is great, but not that way. He just isn't my type. I'm not sure what it is, but there's something that doesn't do it for me. Although, now that I think of it, we do have a lot in common…" She paused to gauge Chantelle's reaction. "Just teasing you. He's all yours."

"And you can rest assured I'll stay away from George."

"Gee, thanks."

In another part of the alley, the men were standing around talking too.

"Justin, do you really trust this guy?" George looked for confirmation. He had felt safe around the stranger, and exhausted.

"I do. If that counts for anything," Nagesh answered before Justin got the opportunity. "I don't think he'd run us around like this just to lay a trap to get us captured. It wouldn't make sense."

"Maybe there's a reward," George answered.

"If there was, it would have been easier for him to simply point us out and be done with it," Nagesh disagreed.

"In the crowd he'd likely have to share the reward. Alone in the alley, he'd have it all to himself," George countered.

"I don't think he's setting us up," Justin interrupted the other two men. "I think he truly wants to help. I sense that he has something against UbiquiMed."

George looked around, observing the alley dead-ended to his left. "Hopefully you're right. Nowhere to run in here."

"He should be back by now, shouldn't he?" Nagesh paced as he asked.

"Soon, I'm sure." Justin tried to allay their fears.

"Quiet!" Chantelle half yelled, half whispered, hearing a noise out on the street in front of their alley.

Justin motioned to everyone to duck down behind trash cans to hide. He edged toward the entrance of the alley, positioning himself to get a look to the street without making his presence known.

Justin pressed his body tightly against the old brick wall and leaned around the corner. Two police transports idled in the streets, blue and red lights flashing. The window was down on one, and the officers were questioning their Good Samaritan. They'd get their answer shortly on whether they could trust the man or not. If he was turning them in for a reward, now was the time.

The street conversation continued for about thirty seconds, concluding with the cruiser windows closing. Seconds later, the transports sped off in different directions. The man continued to walk past the alley.

Justin signaled to the others that they could come out of hiding.

"Well, he didn't turn us in and he had the chance."

"But where did he go? He was just on the street!"

"Over here." The man came up from behind them, from the dead end of the alley. "I had to walk past the alley and enter from an old building. Otherwise, I may have arisen suspicion and they might have followed me into the alley."

"Did you get the thing to kill the transmitters?" George asked.

"Thing? Is that a technical term, George?" Kiara teased her teammate.

"Yes. Right here." The man pulled out a five inch metallic gun-like object from his pocket. He held it up against Nagesh's neck, who instinctively flinched and moved away from the stranger.

"It won't hurt. Come here." The man pulled Nagesh by the arm, forcing the device up against his neck. A slight buzzing sound preceded a yelp from Nagesh. The man pulled the device away from Nagesh and said, "Well, it might hurt a bit. Who's next?"

With Nagesh still wincing and rubbing his neck, Kiara stepped forward, followed closely by Chantelle.

"No need to push, ladies. I'll get you all zapped."

He finished the procedure on all of them and put the device neatly back in his pocket. "I've got to conceal this, as I'm not supposed to have it." He smiled and looked up at them. "But I guess if I get caught with the group of you, it wouldn't matter anyway. Let's get out of here."

# 30 *Spaghetti*

George felt like a mouse in a maze trying to find an elusive piece of cheese. The zigging and zagging made his profusely perspiring head spin. Finally, the group arrived at the man's apartment.

"Couldn't we have just come straight here? They can't track us now!" George once again panted as he protested.

"You guys still stick out in those clothes. The detours were necessary. Are you hungry? I thought I'd whip up some spaghetti."

"Sounds great. I've never had it." Enthusiasm exuded from Kiara's voice.

"You've never had spaghetti?" Their host looked around, surprised as each one of them shook their heads no. "Let me get it started, then we can talk while we eat. The washroom is down the hall if anybody wants to clean up a little. The towels and washcloths are in the vanity under the sink, in the far left drawer."

"Washcloths and towels? Do you actually still use water for washing?" Justin looked scared at the prospect.

"For washing up, yes. I have a sonic shower though," the man replied.

Justin let out a sigh of relief.

Dale J. Moore

The man went to the kitchen to prepare dinner. Nagesh followed him to see how this new meal was prepared. The others queued up for the washroom. Within twenty minutes, Nagesh set the table and the man brought the pots of pasta and sauce to the table. Setting the bowls down and turning back to the counter, he stepped on Bob's tail. The loud cry from Bob startled the guests.

"You have a cat!" Kiara bent down to pet it. Chantelle ran over to see it and the guys all strained for a peek.

"Never seen a cat before, right?"

"What's her name?" Chantelle asked.

"Bob. And he's not my cat. I'll explain in a few minutes." The man scooped a bottle of red wine from a nearby loaded rack. The girls returned to the table, Bob having received the amount of required attention.

"Let me guess, you guys haven't tried wine before?"

Again, a blank look around the table.

"No alcohol of any type, actually," Kiara replied.

"I heard all this stuff about your strict diets, daily exercise regimens, and the best research equipment on the planet." He then looked at George. "So I thought you guys would be in perfect physical shape."

George blushed a little and looked down at his plate.

"Where'd you hear all this?" Justin asked curiously. The man knew much more about them than would be normal. "And by the way, who are you anyway?"

"I'm sorry. I forgot that I didn't introduce myself. I'm in hiding myself, so I'm careful about talking to people." The man passed the pasta to his left, having put a heap on his plate.

"Great, a crook!" Nagesh put his hand to his forehead like he was nursing a headache. "We get rescued by a crook."

"I'm not a crook." The man picked up the serving dish which held his homemade sauce and meatballs. "But I am supposedly dead." He scooped out some sauce and slowly engulfed the steaming stack of noodles. He held the pause for another few seconds while capturing a few meatballs before rolling them to the summit of his spaghetti mountain. He passed the sauce bowl to his left, then continued speaking. "My name is Bruce Templeton. I'm a newscaster, sort of. I work, or at least used to work, in the building you were looking for. I was the host of the 'Such is Life' show you mentioned. That's why I stayed close by after giving you directions."

"I knew I recognized you!" Justin pointed at him with his knife, before realizing it looked threatening and withdrawing it.

"You guys got to watch my show there?" Bruce's widened eyes showed his surprise.

"Not really. I had to go around security protocols," Justin said.

"What do you mean, you *used* to be the host?" Chantelle asked, placing a small amount of noodles on her plate.

"I'm dead, remember?"

"You look very good for being dead," she replied.

"Thanks. I feel okay too."

"So, why are you dead, so to speak?" George asked.

"I ticked off the wrong people at UbiquiMed. I did a number of stories parodying them, and making fun of their CEO, Mr. Antonelli. I guess I hit a nerve. His top security guy, Solomon Reynolds, sent goons that waited until I entered my apartment building then burnt the place down. Luckily I escaped, with Bob here, unlike a number of other poor souls in my building. I was cat-sitting Bob for an elderly neighbour who's out of town. Thank God – she would have never made it out of there."

Justin almost choked on his pasta.

"You know Solomon0214?"

"That's why you're hiding." George's words came out sloppily, having shoved a large quantity of food into his mouth just prior to speaking.

"Exactly. I figure if they think I'm dead, they won't try to kill me again. This apartment is my safe house, for emergencies. So how did you guys get out of UbiquiMed? And why?"

"There were too many lies surfacing in the past few weeks. And your story was the trigger for me."

"What story are you talking about? Remember, I said I did a lot, and I mean *a lot* of stories about UbiquiMed. They are the nation's largest medical company, and their head offices are here in the Bay area."

"About my parents' kidnapping, of course!"

Bruce almost spit out his spaghetti, covering his mouth with his cloth napkin. His eyes watered as he swallowed and laughed loudly. "You mean you broke out because you heard me say your parents were kidnapped?"

"Yes, what's so funny?" Justin raised his voice, visibly upset that Bruce was laughing.

"You really don't know about our show, do you?" He only waited for a few seconds, before finishing his thought. "It's a parody. We make fun of things. Make up stories to make people laugh."

"And kidnapping is funny?"

"The reasons we stated for the kidnapping were funny... that a woman kidnapped them because her husband didn't die and leave her a fortune."

The others at the table laughed. At first Justin remained upset, then realized the humour of the situation. Still blushing, he replied, "Solomon threatened my parents' safety, so I thought it was real. I guess it does sound crazy that they'd be kidnapped by outraged spouses."

"But we followed him for other reasons," Kiara said. "We know they are lying to us. We just weren't planning to take off, but when Justin provided the opportunity, we took it."

"And I just followed Kiara. She's my boss," George meekly added.

Chantelle looked across the table and smiled at Kiara, who gave her a scowl back.

"Yeah, we know the world is different than the violent, war ravaged, politically unstable picture that they painted," Kiara said.

"Well, maybe fifteen years ago it was like that. But certainly not now, as you can see."

"Yet people are still killing people." Nagesh was still leery of their host.

**191**

"People will always kill people," Bruce sighed. "It's in our DNA. The defensive mechanism will always surface when we are threatened. It's who we are."

"But what we saw today was so peaceful, and the Orchid conference looked so peaceful."

"Yes, it did. I've got it recorded. Do you want to watch it? I can give you more background on some of the people you see in it. But it is about an hour long."

Chantelle had just stood up to take her plate to the kitchen. "An hour? We only got to see about ten minutes."

"Ten minutes? We just saw about five minutes, if that." They looked at Kiara as she spoke. "I only saw them introduce the three of you, and then the broadcast was cut off."

From the kitchen Chantelle replied, "Oh you missed the best part! They had our parents on stage and introduced them. They all looked so proud. It was great!"

"It would have been better if we were together in person." Nagesh echoed Justin's thought from the day of the event.

Bruce spoke instructions to his FID, getting the press conference set up for viewing. The living room was arranged for watching the expansive FID, and the group spread out amongst the comfortable couches and chairs. When the screen began showing the outside press conference, the sound came from all around. Chatter came from speakers behind them, as if they were sitting in the audience waiting for the press conference to begin. There were background sounds of bird calls that were so realistic it was tempting to look up to see if they were actually flying around the room.

"That's Mr. Antonelli. I assume you all know who he is?" Bruce looked around to nodding heads. "He's been the main target of my show's jokes and ridicule."

George, who sat closest to the screen, leaned forward. "So you think he ordered his thugs to kill you?"

"I'm not sure if it was him directly, or Reynolds took it upon himself. At least I've narrowed it down from the slew of presidents that run the company today."

"You mean he doesn't run it anymore?"

"He's still the CEO and ultimately in charge. He's involved in making big decisions, no doubt. But as for the day-to-day management, no, he hasn't run it for about three or four years. He likely should have turned the day-to-day operations over a few years before that, but like most CEOs, he's a power freak."

The screen continued to show Mr. Antonelli's opening remarks. They'd all seen this part from their rooms at UbiquiMed. A minute later, the recovered patients came on. Bruce kept talking.

"You know, I thought this cure was all smoke and mirrors at first. I mean, how long have we been trying to cure cancers, and suddenly, when the government is in talks to drastically slash UbiquiMed's control of the medical industry, along comes this cure? It seemed too well timed to be real. My associates and I tracked down the Lees and Hamptons to verify their stories weren't just made up by UbiquiMed."

"Yes, the cure is real alright. We worked a long time on it. Variation after variation, then one day, there it was." Justin looked over at Nagesh and Chantelle, sharing the credit with them.

"Do you know how amazing this is? That's why you guys are celebrities. Your faces are on billboards all around town."

"Billboards?" Chantelle blushed as she spoke, surprised by the thought in spite of seeing a fifteen foot image of herself earlier in the day.

"Yeah, it's amazing. One good thing that came out of the Dark Years was an acknowledgement that developers of knowledge and those that make lives better, such as yourselves, are the real celebrities in the world. Not baseball players, or actresses, or a rich person's daughter for simply being rich and blowing the family fortune in preposterous ways. Although there still is a certain fascination with that kind of news, and I use that term very loosely, it's not the huge business that it used to be. Thank God."

"But billboards?"

"It's also advertising, so don't get too big of a head. Did you guys meet the Lees or Hamptons?"

"No, at least I didn't." Nagesh looked at his team members. "I haven't met a single patient. We're just scientists, not doctors."

"We could be doctors though. We all have the training," Justin added.

Bruce was dumbfounded. He looked at the group, then pointed to the screen as he spoke. "So you haven't met *any* of the people you've cured? Not a one?"

"Nope. Although we did run into that guy today whose father was cured," Justin said, recalling the earlier incident.

"Yeah, that did feel good, didn't it?" Nagesh smiled remembering it too.

Kiara put her hand on Chantelle's shoulder beside her. "To tell the truth, I thought I was going to cry. You should have seen the way he hugged you guys. It was like he was holding onto a parent he hadn't seen in ten years."

"I just thought it was a little creepy," Chantelle replied.

Nagesh defended the man. "He meant well. I think he just got carried away when it came to hugging a pretty young lady like you."

"Look -- there you are!" Kiara jumped up and pointed to the screen as the three of them appeared. "This is where it cut off for me. What's next?"

Chantelle didn't wait for the others to answer. "They introduce our parents. That's when I thought I was going to cry."

Suddenly Kiara screamed out loud. "What are *they* doing there?!?!"

Justin looked at Kiara oddly and replied, "Those are my parents. Do you know them?"

"Ah, yeah. Those are my parents!" She fell backwards onto the couch as she spoke, bumping against Chantelle as she did.

George smiled, pleased with this revelation. "Then you two are brother and sister!"

"Are you sure you're not a rocket scientist, to have figured that out?" Nagesh teased him.

"Rocket science is easy," George replied.

Bruce looked at Justin and Kiara. They both sat staring at each other, not knowing what to say. "Obviously you were right, Justin, about UbiquiMed not telling you guys the truth! I can't believe they kept this kind of thing from you two. Didn't your parents ever say anything?"

"No. Well they might have tried to. Our calls always had the appearance of bad reception, but I'm sure now that UbiquiMed disrupted the transmissions," answered Justin.

"I've got a brother. I knew there was something about you, but couldn't put my finger on it," Kiara said.

The press conference went on in the background, but none of them were watching it. They just looked at each other.

Bruce paced back and forth, his hand on his head in disbelief. He broke the momentary silence. "We've got to get this story out there. I mean the whole UbiquiMed pack of lies and deception. The treatment that you guys have received over the years! This will blow the roof off UbiquiMed and their bids for continued funding. How I get this broadcast without getting killed for real will be the hard part."

# *31* *Breakfast*

Bruce Templeton's hideout was located in an older building, but its mid-twentieth century exterior betrayed the modern, spacious interior. When the old cement and brick structure first came to life to house its original tenants, the apartments were quite modest. Most of them were small one or two bedroom apartments, with very tight quarters in the kitchen area, and only a small living room. Each floor originally consisted of ten apartments. Over the years, the apartments became fewer and larger. Today, each floor held two units. A single unit consumed each of the top three floors. Bruce's master bedroom was likely the size of one of the original two bedroom apartments. He also had two other bedrooms, a very spacious, well appointed kitchen, dining area, games room, and of course the large entertaining area the group occupied while watching the UbiquiMed press conference. This residence was the last thing anyone would ever picture as a 'hideout.'

The girls spent the night occupying one of the spare bedrooms, where a king size bed left them plenty of room. George and Nagesh slept in the other guest room, which had two smaller beds. Justin crashed on the couch, although Nagesh offered to sleep there. George made no similar offer.

The five UbiquiMed escapees all woke up at 7:00 hours, like they had for most of their lives. Even George was up, annoyed that he couldn't get back to sleep when he didn't need to be awake. They were all greeted in the kitchen by Bruce, Bob the cat, and the wondrous smells of a freshly cooked breakfast. The aromas quickly changed George's attitude about staying awake. Bruce had put out quite a spread, anxious to please his guests.

"What *is* that smell? It's incredible!" George followed his nose to a plate with strips of somewhat fatty meat on it.

"Bacon. The one plate is crispy, the other is cooked less, so it's juicier. Which do you prefer, George?"

"I don't know," George replied.

"I know," Bruce said, "you've never had bacon before."

George reached his hand forward to grab a strip from the 'crispy' plate, but his hand was quickly slapped by Kiara. George gave her a 'what gives' look.

"Use a fork. You don't live alone anymore, remember? We don't want you touching our food with your fingers."

"My fault," Bruce interjected, "I forgot to put out serving forks." He stepped between the two combatants, placing a fork on each of the plates before stabbing one into the top of the stack of pancakes. Bruce also nudged a large serving spoon into a large bowl of strawberries.

Justin looked at the spread. "This all looks great, but you didn't need to go to this much trouble."

"No trouble. Besides, I bought way too much stuff the other day. I wasn't sure how long I'd be cooped up here, so I loaded up the fridge and cupboards. Sit down, eat."

None of them needed a second prodding. Even though they all over-ate at last night's spaghetti dinner, they ate like they hadn't eaten in a week. Was it the excitement of their ordeal, or perhaps all the new foods?

Since he ate earlier, and now everyone else sat occupied eating, Bruce was free to talk.

"So, I woke up early this morning to come up with a plan."

"Was that before or after you whipped up this feast?" Nagesh asked. "So what time did you actually get up?"

'Four. Normal for me, really," Bruce said.

George almost finished swallowing a mouthful of pancake before speaking.

"Why do you get up so early? I thought 7:00 hours was bad."

"I have my best creative thoughts when I first wake up. This gives me time to spend a few hours jotting them down, in preparation for our daily script meeting."

Justin appreciated Bruce's comments. He often found his best ideas came with the start of his morning sonic shower. "So, what's the plan?"

"The plan is to get your story recorded and then broadcast for everyone to hear."

"And what about my parents?" Justin asked.

"*Our* parents," Kiara corrected her brother.

"Our parents," Justin smiled at his sister, still getting used to the idea. "What about our parents?"

"I'm sure they are fine. UbiquiMed likely hasn't told them that you've escaped, except…" Bruce left his thought hanging in air.

"Except what?" Kiara asked.

"Well, since you guys are missing, UbiquiMed would have gone to their homes looking for you. They may have them in custody, questioning them."

Kiara looked at Justin and pleaded, "But they don't know anything! I hope you didn't get them in trouble!"

"I'm sure UbiquiMed knows that by now and has let them go. UbiquiMed wouldn't tell your parents that you were missing. It wouldn't be in their best interest. Reynolds probably has your parents under surveillance though, so I don't think it would be wise for either of you to go anywhere near them. I'll get some private detective to watch their place and report back. That way we'll know they are unharmed. Okay?" Bruce looked first at Kiara, who gently nodded her agreement, then he looked at Justin, who did the same as his new sibling.

"Good. I've got some contacts to make today to set up the recording session. I know some people that I can trust. In the meantime, I want you guys to huddle up and make some notes." Bruce turned, reaching toward a stack of papers on the counter. He couldn't quite reach it, and had to jump his chair over a few inches to grasp the pile. "I put together some questions that will be a good starting point. Try to answer them as a group, so that I don't have to compile them later. You'll likely learn a lot about each other and your individual experiences." Bruce handed a paper to each of them. He then got up and threw on a hooded sweatshirt.

"Where are you going?" Nagesh asked.

"I told you, I've got some contacts to make."

"Why don't you just use your FID?" Nagesh pointed toward the entertainment centre as he spoke.

"I can't. I'm dead, remember? In-person contact is best in this situation. Even these people will be surprised to see me."

Dale J. Moore

# 32 *The Letter*

In his years in the entertainment business, Bruce had made many professional acquaintances. Most of them he didn't trust. Most of them were only looking out for themselves. Bruce should know – he'd acted that way for most of his years in broadcasting. He pissed off more than a few people in the process, and rarely did he even care. It was all part of the game. He'd always believed important people have important problems and interesting lives. Unimportant people have unimportant problems and uninteresting lives. Why should he care about uninteresting lives? There's no story in that. Bruce was so focused on the lives and issues of powerful people at the top, that he felt it below him to even acknowledge the common, everyday person, often acting outright rude to fans on the street.

In the last two years or so though, he'd experienced some kind of professional epiphany, and started to treat those around him as other people, not as obstacles or vehicles to his success. It was a difficult transition at first. It disturbed Bruce to find the world indeed did not revolve around him, and that people's lives went on when he was not around them. To see a key grip or cameraman as someone with their own life, own story, own issues, and feelings was initially unsettling to him. These previously unimportant, uninteresting people actually had fascinating perspectives on the 'important and interesting' people. Bruce could see how the media influenced their opinions, but was pleasantly surprised that they saw through a lot of the crap peddled on network broadcasts. He also discovered the amazing sense of humour many of the crew possessed.

It took many, many months, but Bruce no longer felt the need to be the centre of attention at parties, galas, and other functions. He was still more than happy to oblige anyone who wanted him to take centre stage, but it didn't bother him if he didn't – at least not that much. He became willing to check his ego at the door instead of inflating it at the door.

As part of this new found compassion, or at least awareness of other people, he became friends with some of the crew on "Such is Life." He even found himself having lunch with them from time to time. Bruce of a few years ago would have rolled his eyes at such a thought. Of course, he was such an unapproachable jerk back then that no one 'below' the on-camera team or the director would dare ask.

While his crew wasn't best of friends with him, they were friends. He knew their hobbies, their political views, and even remembered the names of some of their wives. Years ago, Bruce would have hit on all the wives, likely had brief affairs with a few of them, and not remembered the women's names. Now, the crew was as close as he had to family or friends, next to Emmaline of course. But he wasn't dragging her into this. Plus she didn't have access to the camera equipment like Larry did.

Bruce knew he couldn't just walk into the studio and ask Larry or anyone else to help him. Dead people generally cause a stir if they are seen walking about, and he wanted to fly under the radar on this one. He decided he'd stick a note in an envelope and pay some Joe a few bucks to run it into the building. An initial rendezvous point would be needed as part of his plan. Someplace discreet, obviously, but not too far from the studio so Larry could slip away unnoticed. He would write the letter in some sort of code in case it was intercepted; yet include some details so that Larry would come. Bruce deliberated for some time on the message, but he came up with the right words and location to put his plan in motion.

Across the street from the studio in Union Square, he quickly scouted out people and found a messenger. The plaza also gave him an ideal vantage point to monitor the letter's delivery. The security guard took the envelope from the rented courier, who followed Bruce's instructions perfectly by simply handing the letter over and turning away. The tall female guard watched the man leave the building before she held the envelope under a scanner to detect anything suspicious. Opening the envelope, she unfolded the letter and swiftly read it before placing it back to its delivery state. The woman then turned and tossed the envelope onto the internal mail cart. So far, so good. Bruce figured Larry would get the mail within a couple of hours. The time for the meeting was planned between rehearsals and the broadcast, when Bruce knew there was an hour or so that the crew had for lunch.

Before his sudden death, Bruce was enjoying a journalistic high that he hadn't felt in years. He loved the work he was doing with 'Such is Life.' Every day provided a challenge to come up with fresh material for his satire. The fast pace of a daily broadcast invigorated him. The mental workout required for each broadcast would be exhausting to some people, but injected Bruce with energy and vitality. The only drawback to the show was its reputation. Stuck in his head was a quote from a major media site, which referred to the show as "a fun, satirical look at the news; a stark contrast to real journalism." Real journalism. Two words that haunted Bruce throughout his success. Roy was a real journalist, covering real stories that mattered. Bruce was a jester, making fun of real stories that mattered. The UbiquiMed story could be his chance to break a real story. To earn his stripes with something serious. He wanted, no needed, to show the world that he was more than the class clown. He wanted to prove to his former mentor Roy that his teaching had paid off, and that Bruce had the stuff to cut it. Mostly, he wanted to prove to himself that he could do it. Bruce also knew the need to protect himself, so another errand was necessary before heading to the meeting place.

# *33* *Rendezvous*

Back at the hideout, the ideas were written down and collected. The group began weeding out duplicate comments, and at the same time organizing the sequence. This proved more difficult than expected. Nagesh and Chantelle looked to Justin for leadership, while George looked to Kiara for the same. It was natural that they followed the team structure that they had lived every day. Justin and Kiara were comfortable in this role when it came to science, but anxiety crept through both of them over such a literary task. Justin always passed the necessary evil of report writing to Nagesh. This seemed like the perfect time to follow that pattern.

"Nagesh, let's think of this as a report to UbiquiMed. You're always so good at reports that I think you should lead this writing exercise."

Nagesh looked at the others. "Anybody else want this?" He paused only briefly and it was obvious that no one else did. "Fine. But I'm just letting you guys know, I'm not good. I just suck less than Justin does at it. Besides, I don't hate it nearly as much as he does."

"No argument from me." Justin patted him on the back to say thanks.

With Nagesh at the helm, the work progressed much quicker. While most of the work was serious, they did exchange a few laughs over some of their naivety toward the real world as they were finding out about it. Justin and Kiara would exchange glances from time to time, both still trying to get used to the thought of having a sibling. After a couple of hours, George went to work searching the refrigerator for food that could be turned into lunch. Having never prepared a meal in their lives, none of them had a clue how to cook anything, but had more material for their notes. The group concurred that sandwiches were the safest course of action for lunch, so George started pulling out ingredients and spreading them across the counter.

About the same time that the five of them took a break to eat, Bruce moved into place to meet Larry. There was an old-style laundromat near the broadcast centre that he settled on for a meeting place. He didn't want any place public like a restaurant, since he frequented all of them within a few kilometres and was likely to be recognized. Bruce considered a nearby small convenience store, but remembered they'd installed security cameras everywhere due to a rash of problems last year. He wanted to avoid anyone's surveillance.

A row of chairs stretched out across the back of the laundry. Bruce picked a chair in the middle, sat down, and unfolded the free entertainment paper he grabbed from the box just inside the door. The paper held more advertising than entertainment, but that was irrelevant. He wanted something to hide behind; and to spy over. There were only a few people doing laundry this morning. A very young lady of Asian descent sat on a chair in the middle of the room, gently pushing a small stroller back and forth. He wasn't sure if the baby inside was sleeping or not, but there was no crying and that was a good thing where he was concerned. The other current client of the establishment was an elderly man. The man slowly and meticulously folded a recently dried stack of undershirts on a table. The well dressed gentleman wore a wedding ring, but to Bruce the man appeared to be a widower. No sign of women's clothing could be seen in the basket of cleaned articles. The man just stared blankly at his shirts as he folded them, like his loss was recent. Bruce felt sorry for the man, but in an odd way he was envious of what the man must have had when she was alive. He'd never understood this reaction until Emmaline came along.

The door opened and Bruce instinctively raised the paper to cover most of his face. He'd put on a hat when he left in the morning, so only a portion of his eyes were visible to the new arrival. Larry stopped in the doorway for a moment before grabbing a paper himself. He casually strode to the back of the laundry and sat down three chairs away from Bruce.

Larry opened his paper as well before speaking.

"I nearly fell off my chair when I got your letter."

"I'm glad you figured it out."

"I knew it was you as soon as I read it. I haven't had a conversation with anybody else about creating a UbiquiMed testicle transplant centre due to them falling off from the Orchid cure. If you hadn't put the date on it, I likely would have thought I'd received a letter from the grave."

"Obviously I'm not dead, and I don't want to be. UbiquiMed is after me, so we have to keep this brief."

**209**

"Sure. What can I do for you?"

"I need you to film something for me."

"It doesn't involve anything illegal does it? I've got to think about Jane and the kids you know."

"No, it's not illegal. It may be dangerous, but it could win us both Nobel prizes, or whatever they give to people these days for exposing major cover-ups."

"I hope it's not a bullet they give them," and he laughed at his own joke. "I don't know. It's about UbiquiMed, isn't it?"

"Yes. I've got five of their most brilliant scientists in hiding. You know those infected researchers they are searching for?"

"I take it they aren't infected."

"No. It's actually Justin Lucas and his team."

"Wow! That's huge! … But why the cover-up?"

"That's what I need you for. They've got to tell their story. I don't want to be rude, but this meeting has gone on too long already. Will you help me? Tonight? I only need you for an hour. Tops. Promise. I can pay you very well. I'm sure you and Jane could use some extra cash."

"That's for sure. Okay. When and where?"

"Tonight. Twenty-three hundred. Basement of Grace Cathedral. Go around back to get in. And thanks, Larry. It means a lot to me."

Bruce got up and left first, keeping his head down during his exit from the laundry. Larry stayed seated. He wondered just what he was getting into, but respected Bruce. He also trusted the man. He just hoped it wouldn't be with his life.

## 34 *Lights, Camera, Action*

Everyone was relieved to see Bruce return safely to the apartment. George was especially happy, sensing it meant a fresh cooked meal.

"So how'd it go? Did you meet your guy?"

"Larry. Yes. We met. Everything is set for tonight at twenty-three hundred hours. How are things on your end?"

Nagesh stepped forward with a freshly printed script. "Hope you don't mind us using your computer system."

"No, not at all. So who's reading it?"

Kiara stood beside her brother and put his arm around him. "Justin and I will read it. We figured it would bring the most clout to have his familiar face starting it."

"But the thought of reading to a camera makes me nervous ..." Justin added.

"So I'm going to read most of it after he starts," Kiara finished.

Bruce smiled. "Good idea. And don't worry. It doesn't have to be polished. Just be yourselves. Do you want to rehearse it first?"

"We already did," Kiara replied.

Bruce looked at the siblings. "Well, which one of you wants to read it to me?"

George grabbed the script from Bruce's hands. "How about I read it to you while you prepare dinner?"

They all laughed at George's obvious ploy to get Bruce started on dinner, and probably to do some sampling too. Bruce agreed and they moved to the kitchen.

The apartment air filled with the smell of fresh garlic sautéing, as Bruce set to cooking. George was having trouble concentrating on his reading and got his hand slapped a couple of times as he acted like a kid by trying to sneak a taste. Bruce suggested a couple of very minor changes, which George hand wrote neatly onto the script. As the reading came to a completion, so did the dinner preparations.

"Garlic Fettucine Alfredo with Shrimp. Enjoy!"

The group all took their places at the table and began to eat.

"This is soooo good!" George commented with his eyes firmly closed, savouring the tastes that arose his palate. A chorus of 'uh hmms' followed from the full mouths around the table.

"I'm glad you're enjoying it. So, Justin and Kiara, I had George mark up a few minor changes. No changes to the content or message. I just suggested you move one topic in front of another for better effect. I think it's great. You guys all did a fantastic job. It's pretty scary stuff to me though. I think this is going to shock a number of people."

Nagesh nodded his thanks. "You mean this will be more shocking than you coming back to life?"

"Yeah, that might surprise a few people too. But this is … well it's just amazing."

Justin had noticed Bruce put a small package on the table by the door when he returned from his meeting with Larry. He didn't ask Bruce at the time about it, but figured now was a good time.

Looking toward the package and pointing his hand in that direction as he spoke, Justin asked "Did Larry give you something at the meeting?"

"Oh no, he didn't. That's just a little insurance policy. I'll show you after the filming tonight. Anybody want seconds?"

After cleaning up from dinner, they flopped around Bruce's entertainment area to watch a couple of recorded broadcasts of 'Such is Life.' Unfortunately they didn't get many of the jokes, the group having no awareness of current events or people in the news. Bruce spent an hour trying to explain his jokes before he gave up and called up an action thriller for them to watch. He explained to them that none of it was real and that it was all simulated on computers or in a movie studio. They all enjoyed the movie much more than his own show, but Bruce didn't mind. He just marveled watching these young men and women experiencing a movie for the first time. He wondered how marvellous it must seem to them.

George spoke first after the movie.

"So none of those guys really died?"

"That's right. It's all pretend. Like when you were a kid." Bruce looked at five blank stares. "Okay, maybe not when you were kids, but when I was kid. We played make-believe all the time."

"I could see how that could be fun. You know, pretending to be somebody else," Chantelle smiled.

Nagesh replied, "You mean like wearing a disguise and darting around alleys like a spy?"

"I guess we do have some experience pretending after all," Chantelle laughed.

"And we'd better get used to wearing disguises for a while," Justin replied.

Bruce looked at the clock.

"We'd better get ready to go. I don't want to leave Larry waiting. He's nervous about the whole thing."

As they walked through another maze of streets and alleys, up and down hills, Bruce explained his plan.

"I'm going to take you guys to a small building across the alley from the back of the church. You'll wait there until I signal you that it's safe."

"When it's safe?" George sounded and looked nervous, fumbling with his own fingers.

"Yes, the UbiquiMed bad guys. Remember, George?" Kiara sounded more than a little condescending in her words to him.

"Yes. When it's safe," Bruce continued, "I'll wave you over and we can get right to recording. I want to get in and get out. I want to send Larry on his way as soon as possible and get you back under wraps in the apartment."

Bruce looked both ways in the alley, then took a few running steps toward the church before coming to a sudden stop. He turned and ran back, reaching into his pocket as he approached Justin. Bruce held up a key and placed it in Justin's hand.

"Just in case."

The two exchanged eye contact for a few seconds, but no words. Bruce placed his hand on Justin's shoulder, holding it there for a moment before turning and entering the darkness of the alley. A few seconds later, Bruce disappeared into the church basement through the back door entrance.

The dimly lit stairwell to the downstairs led to a dark church hall. From visiting in the hall for other functions, Bruce knew its layout. A small stage stood at the front, with entrances to both sides covered by old brown curtains. A kitchen area in the back proved useful in drawing functions to the old church and generating much needed funds. This reminded him of the envelope in his pocket. He stopped a few steps downward and retreated back up the stairs to the main church. The donations box was around the corner and he placed the envelope securely inside, thanking God for his open door policy. Bruce hurried back down the stairs.

He didn't want to bother filming on the stage. If no function was planned for the next day, the church usually stored things behind the curtain, typically stacks of chairs or boxes of donations. He didn't want to move things around up there, rationalizing the stage and curtain would make a good backdrop if Larry didn't bring a portable screen to set up behind Justin and Kiara. No doubt he'd have to move a few tables and chairs on the floor, but they would slide around quite easily and quickly on the linoleum tile.

He hadn't visited before when the hall lights were off, but assumed it was an energy conservation measure. Everyone had to do their part he supposed, even churches, although their motivation might have involved conservation of cash too. The light switch. Where was the light switch? He probed the recesses of his mind to remember. Nothing came to mind – recess must be out. Instead, instinct told him to grope around the wall to his right. If that failed he'd go to the left hand wall. Two choices, he figured. A few flat hand touches along the wall was all it took to locate the switch. He flipped it on.

"Good evening, Mr. Templeton. I bet you are as surprised to see us as we were to hear you were still alive." Solomon Reynolds stood there, between two of his goons. Bruce was speechless, but thought to himself how screwed he was. Two weapons pointed at him.

"So you are surprised! Good. Good. It is so rare to see you speechless, Mr. Templeton. Such a treat for us, right, Henry?"

Henry? Bruce thought to himself, who ever heard of a goon named Henry? Sounds more like a tech genius or an escapee from an asylum. He decided it was best to keep his smart remarks to himself though, since Henry held a gun.

"Surprise also means you have no backup. This should be easy."

Bruce looked around, wondering if he had sent Larry to his death along with him. "What did you do with Larry?"

"Not to worry. Your camera man is sitting comfortably at home with his wife, probably counting his money."

"He set me up?" Bruce said it, but couldn't believe it.

"No, you can go to your grave not thinking your friend is a rat. We made him a better offer."

Henry finally spoke. "Yeah, Mr. Reynolds gave Larry two choices: make his wife a poor widow, or keep living and improve his quality of life. I think he chose well." A creepy smile fit for a Halloween mask covered Henry's face, thinking his comment quite clever.

"Tough choice. Okay, I guess I'll just be on my way then," Bruce pointed to the stairwell as he spoke.

"I don't think so. Where are they?" Reynolds asked.

"Who are you talking about?" Bruce feigned ignorance.

"Justin Lucas and the others. Don't waste our time playing dumb. Larry told us about them," Reynolds replied, showing signs of impatience.

"Well, at least after a little persuasion he told us," Henry added.

"Why would I tell you? You're going to kill me anyway."

Reynolds put his hand on his chin, pretending to think over the question. He looked over to his other goon and replied.

"He makes a good point, Karl."

Karl. Now that was a better name for a thug. Just sounds tough. Bruce slowly backed up toward the wall.

"Maybe it will save you some pain," Karl answered.

Reynolds had a disturbing, satisfied smile covering his face. "I was thinking that if you told us we would just shoot you afterward. If you don't tell us, we have to go through all that torture nonsense to get the information. Then we shoot you anyway. So I guess the answer is your choice; die quickly or a slow painful death."

"Well that's at least something to think about..." Bruce put his left hand up to his head, pretending to ponder his situation. It was purely a distraction though, an old magician's trick Roy taught him during a night of heavy drinking. With his right hand Bruce reached back and hit the light switch. He caught Karl and Henry off guard. Bruce spun, running toward the steps.

Shots were fired.

Two shots.

Four shots.

Six shots.

"I think I got him," Henry yelled out.

Karl made his way over and turned on the light. Their target was gone from view.

Bruce ran through the dark toward the stairs. He ascended a few of the stairs before hearing gunfire and acquiring a sharp pain in the back of his leg. He winced, but determined, he continued up the stairs before feeling a second pain in his back. A few more shots rang out, but he managed to get around the bend in the stairs. Bruce touched blood as he put his hand to his back. He was certain his leg was also bleeding.

# 35 *The Message*

The door to the back of the church was faintly illuminated. The group saw Bruce vanish through the entrance and their focus remained on the old steel door as the minutes ticked away. They were relieved to see the lights go on in the basement. Minutes later, however, the shots sent them into a panic. They had never experienced violence.

"I'm going in." Justin looked at the rest of them with a sense of duty and purpose.

Kiara stepped in front of him to stop him.

"No you are not! I just got a brother yesterday. I'm not going to lose him today to some stupid macho attempt to be a hero."

The door to the church basement flung open. A doubled over Bruce fell through it and onto the cement walk.

"I've got to help him!" Justin exclaimed.

Nagesh grabbed Justin's arm, pulling him back.

Kiara stepped in front of Justin and put a hand on his chest.

"How? You've got no weapon. Whoever shot Bruce will be right behind him. You'll get killed too."

Chantelle stepped up beside Kiara.

"She's right you know. You can't help. He gave you a key in case something went wrong. Something went wrong!"

They looked across the alley toward Bruce. He tried to stand up, but clutched his back in pain. He fell to his knees, but straightened up long enough to wave at them to get lost.

"We can't just leave him like that. He's going to die!" Justin yanked his arm in an attempt to free himself from Nagesh's grip. George grabbed his other arm to restrain Justin further.

"Now, Justin! We can't help him. We need to leave right now!" Kiara told him as she put her other hand on his chest too.

Justin looked toward Bruce again, tears falling from his eyes onto Kiara's hands. He knew they were right. They vanished into the dark before Bruce's assailants came through the door.

The trek back to the apartment took much longer than the way to the church, at least mentally. The excitement of telling their story had disappeared, replaced with the despair of seeing their new friend collapsing, bleeding. At one point in the run back, George started to lose it.

"What are we going to do now? UbiquiMed's going to come after us and kill us too!"

Justin responded quickly and strongly. "We are all going to remain quiet until we get back to the apartment. Then we will come up with a plan. No one is going to kill us."

George looked like he was going to reply, but looked at Kiara's glare and knew best to clam up.

As he reached for the lock with the key Bruce had given him, Justin's hand shook uncontrollably. He tried not to let the others notice, but had trouble steadying it long enough to get the key in the hole. Chantelle, close beside him, noticed the shaking. She leaned up close against him to prevent the others from seeing, then held his hand to calm the shakes. The key entered the lock and turned easily, opening the door for the anxious group. Justin looked at Chantelle and said thanks. Kiara noticed how close Justin and Chantelle were standing and couldn't resist a dig she'd heard in the movie last night.

"Get a room, why don't you?"

The remark didn't bother Chantelle, but Justin blushed and pulled away.

After everyone moved inside, Justin shut the door and activated the security system. Knowing that George would be the first to say anything, and most likely to sound panicky, Justin took a pre-emptive step.

"Let's get out some food and drinks. We'll sit around the table to figure out what options we have." Justin assumed food would be a distraction for George and was correct. As the group pulled out an assortment of containers and assembled them in the middle of the table, Justin remembered the parcel left by Bruce. The 'insurance package', as Bruce called it. He picked up the wrapped package and walked over to the table. His hands rotated the package a few times, looking for how it was wrapped and the most efficient way to uncover its contents. Justin sat at the table to open it.

Nagesh stopped putting food on his plate and asked, "What is it?"

"It's the package Bruce left behind. I was just about to open it."

"What do you think it is?"

Justin gave him an annoyed look. "I haven't a clue. And I won't until you let me open it!"

Nagesh shrugged his shoulders, mumbling a wimpy "Sorry."

Justin had the package turned so that the taped side faced upward. He fiddled with the tape for a few seconds before abandoning that method to just tear at the paper. It was much like a child opening a Christmas present in front of his parents, but none of them had that experience to recall either. Tearing the wrap, a folded piece of paper fell onto the table, snapped up by Chantelle as she sat next to Justin. She unfolded it as he finished removing the remnants of paper that covered a small video camera.

"What's the note say, Chantelle?" George's interest had finally swayed from food to the activities at the table.

"I hope this is the 'Sci-Five' reading this note. Get it, the five scientists? Thought it would make a cute by-line. It also likely means that something bad has happened to me, like I'm dead again." Chantelle laughed, but covered her mouth, embarrassed about it. At the same time, a small tear trickled from her right eye. She continued reading.

"Just in case the meeting with Larry went wrong, I used the enclosed camera to record my introduction to your piece. It's not the quality that your story deserves, but there were some things that I had to say and apparently I wouldn't have gotten the opportunity otherwise. I've also included a few basic instructions on how to operate this camera, in case you didn't get the chance to record your message. They are on the back of this sheet, and a second recording disk is included.

**222**

When you are done, make copies of both, then get a set to my friend Roy. His address is also on the back. He's the only one that I can trust to do the right thing. Remember, when you are filming your bit, look straight into the camera and just be yourself. Roy can clean it up before airing it. I know you guys will do well. All the best, Bruce."

There wasn't a dry eye around the table.

Nagesh spoke first after a brief silence. "Let's watch his video."

Kiara, wiping tears from her eyes, replied, "No. I can't. Not now anyway. We need to get our bit recorded, and if I watch his video, I won't be able to compose myself."

Justin had his arm around Chantelle to comfort her as she read the note from Bruce. Now he turned to Kiara and embraced her with both arms.

"You're right. Let's wash up and get the recording done. Nagesh can figure out the video recorder." He looked at Nagesh and smiled. "That'll take you about a minute, eh Nagesh?"

"Maybe less, Justin. When you two are ready, I'll be all set."

Dale J. Moore

# 36 Roy

Recording their message, tears interrupted them many times. Their message, written before Bruce was felled, included a number of references to him. Each mention brought a struggle to fight back the emotional swell, and in some cases the fight was lost. Nagesh simply stopped the recording while they regrouped. It was an experience that would no doubt bond the five of them together forever. Within three hours they had captured about fifteen minutes of material, at least that was Nagesh's estimate. He didn't even want to attempt editing it. They all felt good about the message and that they effectively captured the key points. Nagesh found some extra disks in Bruce's video cabinet and figured out how to make copies of their message and Bruce's message.

The night had rolled without notice into morning. The collective decided they were much too exhausted to watch Bruce's video until after some sleep. Although Bruce's room now lay empty, they stuck to the previous night's sleeping arrangements, including Justin using the couch.

The next morning came sooner than any of them desired, having endured an emotionally exhausting preceding day. Their internal clocks didn't wake them at 7:00 hours per usual. Their conditioning under UbiquiMed proved consistent though. They all woke at 10:00 hours instead, giving them each about six hours of sleep.

They took turns showering and eating breakfast. Since queuing up for showers took longer than eating, the table was cleared before George returned from having the last shower.

Chantelle began talking as George pulled out his chair to sit down.

"I propose that we vote whether to watch Bruce's video now or wait."

George made a banging noise with his chair as he landed down hard onto it. They all looked at him to see if he had broken their host's chair. George looked down at the legs, finding no outward signs of damage. He looked up and asked, "Why do we need to vote? If you don't want to watch it, don't watch it."

"I want to vote. I don't think I can take another session of crying. If you play it, I'll hear it no matter where I go in the apartment," Chantelle replied.

"Go outside for a while," George quipped, lacking any sensitivity.

Justin didn't like where the discussion was headed. "Nobody goes outside, first of all. Second, and more amazingly, I agree with George."

George sat up straight in his chair, puffing out his chest.

Justin continued, "We're all going to see it or hear it eventually. I'd rather watch it in private first, instead of seeing it for the first time in front of a big crowd of people."

Chantelle nodded agreement. "I guess you're right. But why a big crowd of people?"

"I'm going to contact Bruce's friend Roy, as soon as we are done watching Bruce's introduction. I intend to set up a meeting with Roy to get him to edit the two pieces together for us. Then I want him to show it at that big plaza tonight. Bruce said Roy was as big a media star as there ever was. I saw posters about a 'Media Night' there tonight, and thought Roy could use his influence to get our movie shown. I think Bruce would like that."

"Yeah, sounds good." Nagesh's tone wasn't convincing.

"What's wrong with that plan?" Kiara asked.

"Well, let's see," Nagesh replied, "Justin has to find this Roy guy. Then he has to meet with him and convince him of the plan. It's likely risky for Roy, since it got Bruce killed."

Kiara raised her hand, with her first finger sticking up in objection. "We did not get Bruce killed. They tried to kill him before we even met him."

"You're right of course, Kiara," Nagesh apologized. "I'm sorry it came out that way. But it will be dangerous for this Roy guy. Also, Roy will have to do all the editing in a few hours to have it ready for tonight. Plus he has to figure out how to get it shown at this Media Day."

"I know it's a tall order." Justin put both hands on the table in front of him, then stood up to continue. "But it can be done. Bruce had faith in this Roy fellow, and I think we have to as well. You make a good point, Nagesh, about the timing, so I will try to contact Roy right away. Can you guys wait a while before starting to watch Bruce's movie?"

"Of course," Nagesh replied.

Justin grabbed the piece of paper with Roy's contact information on it, copying it to a smaller piece of paper. The large paper went back on the table, while the smaller one found a place in his pocket. He grabbed the key off of the counter and put the disks in his pocket.

"Where are you going?" Chantelle asked.

"I can't contact him from here. If he can't be trusted, they'll track the call back to here. I need to go a few blocks away. I don't know how long I'll be. It will depend if I can meet him right away or not. So don't worry if I'm not back in twenty minutes." Justin picked up some money from a dish by the door and shoved it in his pocket. He'd no doubt need it to place his call. He placed a hand on the doorknob and simultaneously felt a soft hand on his arm. He turned and was pulled into a deep embrace by Chantelle.

"Okay, enough already." Kiara stood a couple of feet away. "Let me give you a hug for luck."

Chantelle looked at her. "I'm not done yet." She then looked into Justin's eyes, then closed her eyes and gave him a long kiss. Kiara stood there speechless. No quick quip was forthcoming. The kiss eventually ended and Chantelle stepped back, looking at Kiara. "Okay, sis, I'm done. For now, anyways."

Kiara walked over and gave Justin a short hug. She slapped a hat on his head before wishing him good luck and locking the door behind him.

Justin left the hideout floating on a cloud. Just days ago he'd imagined just holding this beautiful girl's hand and looking into her eyes. Now she'd kissed him in ways that did some weird things to his mind, and his body. He had to try to block it out for now to get his mission accomplished. They were all counting on him, Chantelle included. He knew Bruce especially counted on him.

The front door of the apartment led onto a busy street. He could see steady foot traffic from his vantage point in the lobby. He peeked at his watch -- likely the lunch crowd by now. A quick look around the first floor showed exit signs at both sides of the building as well as the front door. One of the side exits would most certainly lead to a quieter, less conspicuous exit. Approaching the right side exit, his guess was confirmed. Nobody was walking by the door.

Following Bruce's example, Justin engaged in a weaving pattern through streets and alleys. After a few of these zigs and zags, he started looking for someplace to place his call. A few 'Communication Stations' were visible from the corner where he stood. He examined the location of each, including the direction that each faced and the number of passersby. There was no sign of law enforcement. Justin crossed the street to a station that was facing away from the street, hopefully cutting down on the chance that someone would recognize him. He slipped into the booth, closing the door behind him. An unfamiliar display panel lay in front of him and began speaking to him.

"For your privacy, please ensure the door is completely closed."

Justin tugged on the door handle and heard a click.

"Thank you. Please select the type of communication you wish to enact."

The choices displayed in front of him included text only, voice only, image only, data only, and a myriad of combinations of each. He decided to take a chance and selected voice and image. Justin hoped that his image would help Roy take him seriously, assuming that Roy had seen his face (which seemed plastered everywhere). He also hoped that Roy was not being monitored and that the image would not trigger UbiquiMed sweeping down on his location. He had to take that chance.

A couple of more prompts followed to secure payment, before he finally entered the contact number and the call was initiated. The line rang at the other end. And it rang again. And again.

"Hi, this is Roy."

"Roy, this is Justin Lucas."

"I'm not currently available. Please leave a message after the tone."

An answering system. Great. What should he say?

"Wait ... don't hang up!"

An elderly man's face suddenly appeared on the screen in front of Justin.

"Sorry, but I get a lot of crank calls, being a former journalist who pissed off a lot of people."

"I understand. Bruce said he had the same problem."

"Bruce Templeton? When did you talk to Bruce?"

"Yesterday."

"But he's been dead a week! Are you sure it was him?"

"Absolutely. We need to meet. Somewhere secure. I've got a big story for you from Bruce."

"You're a big story. Nobody's even interviewed you and you're the biggest celebrity there is right now."

"Then you'll meet?"

"Yes. Let me get a crew together."

"No. No crew. We already have a video for you. It's rough, but Bruce tells me you can polish it up in no time."

"Bring Bruce and tell him to meet me where we met for the Kipling story. He'll know where I mean."

"Bruce is dead."

"I thought you said you just met with him."

"We did. He wasn't dead, but now he is."

There was a brief pause on the line.

"Sorry to hear that. I'll send you an address. Memorize it and meet me there in thirty minutes, if that's not too soon. And who's 'we'?"

"I can tell you more when we meet." Justin saw the address come across his screen. "Got the address. See you in thirty minutes."

Justin read the screen, then with a tap of his finger, the screen went blank, erasing the address that was now planted in his mind. One good thing had come from all the zigging and zagging they'd done through the streets in the last twenty-four hours; he'd built a mental map of the area through the many street signs he'd observed, and had a good idea where to go. In case he was being watched, Justin went alone instead of doubling back for the others. As he remembered, there was a small store on the way where he could stop and get a drink. There was time to spare and he wanted to get into viewing range of the address ahead of time to watch who was coming and going.

The brisk walk got his adrenalin pumping even more. The drink was cooling him off but not slowing down his pounding heart. The world might not be the war state that UbiquiMed had him believe, but it was dangerous nonetheless. Bruce had exercised caution and still ended up murdered. Justin had none of the street smarts that Bruce possessed and wondered if he'd live through the day.

Watching the building proved uneventful. He hoped that was a good thing. The only person to come or go was an elderly lady walking her dog. Justin had never seen a real dog and stared at the movements of this creature with curiosity. It was so different from the way Bob moved and acted. As the pet and its master returned to the entrance and started up the stairs, a man slid by her to hold the door ajar. Could this be his man?

Trying to see if it was a trap, Justin waited until a few minutes after the designated time to approach the building. Jogging up the steps, he scanned the list of buzzer numbers and pushed the desired one.

"Can I help you?"

Using his name was not a good idea, so Justin replied "It's Bruce's friend."

"Come up."

Looking over his shoulder to the street, Justin pulled at the door as the lock was released electronically. He stepped inside and tugged the door shut behind him until he heard a click. The apartment number was on the second floor. Stairs were the logical choice, so up he went.

The unit was located right beside the stairwell exit. A quick knock and the door immediately flung open.

"Come in. Quick."

Urgency was evident as Roy pushed the door closed, brushing it against Justin as he did.

"This is indeed a surprise, young man. I have to say that I am honoured to meet you, and I have met Presidents, a Queen, and even a dictator or two."

"Thank you, sir."

"Drop the sir stuff. Just because I'm old enough to be your father ... well, old enough to be your grandfather, doesn't mean you need to call me sir. Roy will do fine."

"Okay, Roy. We have a story to tell. I need your help to edit the story and get it on the screen in Union Square tonight."

"You don't expect much, do you, Justin Lucas?"

Justin slid his hand into his pocket and produced the two disks.

"We've already recorded our story, but it was done on a hand-held unit. We had to cut many times and restart."

"How long is it that you needed two disks?"

"It's not that long in total. One disk is our story, as told by us. It's about fifteen minutes. The other disk is an introduction by Bruce before ... before last night. It's only a couple of minutes."

"There's the 'us' again. Who are you referring to when you say 'us'?"

"There are five of us. I can tell you while you start editing the story."

"Okay. Bruce and I used this hideaway to film and edit a story many years ago. I've got all the equipment here in the apartment. It's a little older now, but it will still do the job for what you need."

"Can you get it done by tonight?"

"I won't know until I see what you've got. Good chance that I can if it's around fifteen minutes."

"What about getting it on the screen tonight?"

"That may be a little tougher, but I do have some friends down there. If this story is as good as Bruce thought it was, it will be worth using all my favours."

# *37* The Story

Editing the film was simultaneously exhausting and exhilarating for Roy. Working on the film made him feel forty-five years old again. He was at the prime of his career back then. Roy hit one big story after another in those days. People came to him with so many stories that he had to turn many good ones down. Considering the restrictions on journalists, particularly him, coming out of the Dark Years, he was lucky to continue his success and popularity. He knew Bruce was in his prime when he died and that this should be his breakthrough story. Roy wanted it to still be that story for Bruce. He was going to make it happen.

The first time Roy watched the two disks, he broke down in tears. He knew he had the material on the two disks to bring down UbiquiMed's empire. This story could be that big. Justin was sent to the other room to allow Roy to work, plus Justin didn't want to see Bruce's video without his friends. After a couple of hours, Roy came out rubbing his eyes.

"Done?"

"Almost. I think you need to get back to your friends. They'll be worrying by now. I'll have it done in another hour or so. We'll meet at the right side stage tonight. Be there ten minutes before show-time. Keep those faces covered up. Sunglasses. Hats. Hoods. I don't care what you do, just don't get yourselves recognized. We need the element of surprise. This won't be as effective if you're tucked away and silenced back at UbiquiMed."

Justin slipped out of the apartment via the back door. Weaving through alleys and side streets, he made it back to Bruce's apartment very quickly. He wondered if Roy knew Bruce's hideout was so close.

"Get the door! Check to see if it's Justin!" Chantelle's pacing back and forth, for what seemed like an eternity, had long made everyone else nervous.

Kiara kept telling her to sit down, repeating over and over that Justin would be okay. The words were as much to convince herself as Chantelle.

A quick check in the monitor and she deactivated security, allowing the door to open without a blaring alarm.

"You made it!" was followed by another hug from Chantelle.

Kiara wanted to break it up before she had to watch them kiss again.

"How'd it go?"

"Great. I think we're in good hands. Everything is set for tonight. At least I hope it is. Roy still had to make some arrangements, but he felt quite sure he could do it."

"How's the video look?" Kiara asked.

"I look good. You look fat."

Justin's teasing invoked a sharp punch in the arm that he wasn't expecting but deserved.

"Acting like brother and sister already," Nagesh laughed at the two of them, inwardly hoping that he had family that he didn't know about. That would be the best thing he could imagine.

George's one-track mind kicked into gear. "I say we eat while we're waiting. No sense going on an empty stomach."

It was Nagesh's turn to tease him. "You are right, George. We should eat. We should eat well. It may be our last meal, so let's eat like royalty!"

"If you're trying to make me lose my appetite, forget it," George replied.

"I somehow figured it wouldn't work," Nagesh laughed again.


Dinner dishes were cleaned and put away neatly. Nagesh found a few more blank disks in Bruce's cabinet, and at Justin's suggestion, he made more copies of their unedited film. Chantelle looked up addresses for each of their parents, writing them on the front of SF-NET envelopes she found. The disks were inserted into each envelope, along with a brief personal letter from each child. They would slide them into the mail on the way to the plaza. It wasn't done for insurance in case their plan failed. It was just done.

They sat closely together to watch Bruce's video. Their friend left an indelible impression with his words. At the end, they got up, cleaned up, and got ready to tell their story.


The streets of San Francisco were always lively at night. The Dark Years had halted this tradition for a few years but couldn't keep the culture from resurrecting it. The crowds were an advantage for blending into, but also increased their chances of someone identifying them. Following Roy's tip, each member of the group was all covered from the neck up as they headed out to the play.

Solomon Reynolds stood, arms crossed, at the back of the assembling crowd in Union Square. The security station was strategically positioned by the main rear entrance. Normally he would not pull duty for an event like this. He despised anything artsy, almost as much as fundraisers or meet and greet appearances for Mr. Antonelli. However, since his boss was on hand for tonight's event, so was he. Solomon's annoyance was tempered by the hope that his five missing scientists might show up at a public gathering like this. He had plenty of extra men around the perimeter. They all received photos of their prey. Mr. Reynolds would escort Mr. Antonelli down the centre aisle to his seat in the front just ahead of show-time, which was fast approaching. Unlike many occasions, Mrs. Antonelli would be accompanying her husband tonight.

Roy was easy for Justin to spot. Roy had made no attempt to cover up. In fact, he was employing the opposite strategy of trying to get recognized by as many people as possible. He was sweet talking every stage hand, actor, and the show's producer.

The group got to within about fifteen feet of Roy then stopped. Roy gestured quickly to let them know he saw them, and to let them know to hold their position. The producer finished talking to Roy, gave him a hug, and went toward the stage. Some music began to play over the speakers that circled the plaza. The crowd started clapping along to the well-known tune. Mr. and Mrs. Antonelli took their seats. Ten seconds later the music stopped. Reynolds headed back to his security post at the apex of the pavilion.

"Hello, San Francisco!" There was some additional applause. "Welcome to Media Night, sponsored by our good friends at UbiquiMed." The emcee motioned towards Mr. and Mrs. Antonelli before continuing. "This is the media's special sneak peak at the new play by San Francisco's own Guillermo Estaban!" A huge picture of the playwright filled the screens around the stage. The producer continued, following a polite round of applause.

"And after the show, Mr. Estaban will answer some previously submitted questions to help you with your kind reviews tomorrow. But first, I have a surprise visitor for you that I'm sure you will enjoy seeing. He is a multiple award-winning journalist. Please welcome our retired friend, Mr. Roy Goodwyn!"

Roy moved into position behind the stage curtain, then walked briskly out to the microphone. He knew this was a tough crowd, having lived their point of view for years. He figured to make his point quickly, before they lost attention and pushed him off stage in favour of the new play.

"Ladies and Gentlemen. Let's just pretend for now that you are ladies and gentlemen." Laughter came from the crowd. He looked back toward the area where he had stood. "Ladies and Gentlemen. I'm proud to introduce you to Justin Lucas and his team of scientists!" Roy motioned to them to come on stage. They took off their hats, hoods, scarves, and sunglasses and approached the microphone. Initially, the crowd was silent. One of the video operators got a close-up of Justin on the large screen and the applause began to grow. The crowd rose to their feet and the ovation erupted.

Reynolds had focused his energy watching the entrances and did not expect Justin Lucas to enter front and centre on the stage. He motioned to teams on both sides of the plaza to head toward the stage. Reynolds himself started down the centre aisle, which had narrowed then collapsed as the crowd continued to stand and jockey for a good view. This impeded his approach, as he had to push his way through the throng.

"Just wave, everyone," Roy quietly instructed the shell-shocked youngsters. He then pushed Justin to the microphone.

"Thank you, everyone. It would mean a lot to us if you would watch this short video that we've put together."

The crowd quieted before Justin spoke, but they remained standing in anticipation of his words. Within seconds of him finishing, the video began to play. Roy's meet and greet with the production staff was paying off (or maybe his payoff was paying off).

A sea of whispers filled the plaza as Bruce Templeton's oversize image filled the screens. Being a professional and expecting this response, Bruce had waited ten seconds before speaking when he filmed it.

"Hello, America. This is Bruce Templeton. As you know, I'm dead. I was dead before I filmed this video, and now I'm likely dead again or I'd be here in person. But that's another story. Many of you know me as the funny guy from 'Such is Life.' Today I'm here to introduce a serious story. I'm here to introduce five of the most brilliant minds in the world, and five of the bravest young people I have ever known. This is the story of five people who have been held prisoners by UbiquiMed since they were three years old." Again he paused for effect. And effect it had. The murmurs had increased in intensity. Roy looked around at some of the plaza police officers who looked agitated but kept from coming on the stage. He spotted Reynolds about halfway down the centre aisle. Bruce's video continued.

"But rather than take my word for it, let's hear it in the words of these amazing scientists." Bruce's face faded slowly and Justin's face appeared. The audience was completely silent. Solomon Reynolds stopped a few rows short of the stage, within a few feet of Mr. Antonelli. Reynolds wanted to shut down the video. He knew though that a riot would ensue and his boss would not be pleased by a public relations fiasco. Reynolds would just have to wait for now. Patience was not his strong suit in situations like this one; when cunning was irrelevant, he preferred brute force.

The video played.

"Hello. My name is Justin Lucas. Since I was three years old, I have lived under San Francisco Bay in an apartment all by myself. I have not seen my parents in person since I was three. Prior to yesterday, I had only been in the same room as another human three times in the past fifteen years. Those were all doctor visits. I had not held another person's hand in almost twenty-two years. I did not know until yesterday that I have a twenty-one year old sister. Let me introduce you to Kiara, another UbiquiMed victim."

"Thank you, Justin. I too, like my brother, have lived as an indentured servant at UbiquiMed since I was three. The others in our group, Chantelle, Nagesh, and George all have the same experiences.

UbiquiMed told us that the entire world was at war, and had been for years. They told us that the only way that we could safely develop medicines was to work in their secure, isolated facilities. They told us that the weapons of war had made the air outside dangerous to breathe. Our location was supposedly top-secret, and that's why we weren't allowed visits from our parents. Every time our parents tried to tell us something on our video links, they were censured. UbiquiMed told us it was due to bad connections caused by the war. We watched our parents age in front of our eyes, yet we knew very little about them, or their values.

What Bruce Templeton didn't tell you is that he was killed by UbiquiMed. First they tried to kill him by burning down his apartment. Then they shot him as he was trying to arrange for us to make this video." The video jumped a bit, the result of Nagesh shutting off the camera while Kiara regrouped from crying. Roy intentionally left it in the video for effect. It worked.

"We were treated fine physically by UbiquiMed. We had a clean place to live with regular meals. We were given the best and newest equipment to perform our research. Any equipment or supplies we needed, we were given." Nagesh zoomed out to include Justin in the shot. He spoke next.

"We succeeded in creating an incredible scientific breakthrough. We just wonder at what cost. Obviously it cost Bruce Templeton his life. It cost us our childhoods. It cost us our teenage years. It cost our parents their children. None of us were told that we would get released at age twenty-five, which by the way, I will be turning this year. We knew of no end to this lonely existence. I have no idea how many other scientists are held captive by UbiquiMed like us. I know that the facility that we escaped from was very large. Bruce told me that the San Francisco location is one of many across the country. It is time to close the on UbiquiMed running our health system. The cost for scientists like me is too great. We hope to continue our research, but as free men and women. Please support our freedom and run this story in your media. Thank you."

The images stopped and the screens went dark. Then a series of large spotlights came to life, illuminating each of the six people on the stage. Writers in the audience crowded toward the stage, yelling out questions.

"Please! Please!" Roy spoke loudly into the microphone. He looked at the UbiquiMed security guards and they no longer looked like they wanted to arrest him. "This film is being distributed electronically to every media outlet in the country as I speak. I've set up interview times for tomorrow and a schedule is included with the video. For tonight, we thank you for no questions and the time to rest for a busy day that lies ahead. Thank you."

Roy put his hand on Justin's back to direct him off stage. There were a few questions hollered at them, but they kept walking without answering them. As they neared the stage curtain, a long haired man with a moustache was assisted onto the stage by a woman. He awkwardly climbed onto the stage near the podium. He grabbed his back to straighten up as he leaned toward the microphone.

"I've got a question," the man's voice bellowed across the stage. "Who's your witness that UbiquiMed killed Bruce Templeton?"

Solomon Reynolds could no longer contain himself. He jumped up on the stage from the centre row. He headed straight to the man, yanking the microphone out of the stand when he got there.

"That's right! Who's your witness? You can't just come up here and slander the good name of UbiquiMed and Mr. Antonelli without any proof. It's all lies I say!"

The man who'd been pushed away grabbed back the microphone from a surprised Solomon Reynolds. The man removed his moustache, yanking off his flowing wig.

"Bruce!" The scientists yelled, along with declarations from the crowd.

"I'm the witness, Reynolds."

"But how?" Reynolds asked. "I saw you dead on the ground."

"Yes, how?" Kiara asked.

"Right after I signaled you guys to leave, the priest hit the spotlights at the back of the church. He thought the noise was coming from the alley and wanted to scare off any trouble back there. I was unconscious. The goons took off, assuming they had done their job, and figuring cameras were hooked up to the lights. They were right about the cameras. We've got perfect shots of them leaving the scene – with you, Mr. Reynolds. The priest brought me in and got me to the nearby hospital for treatment. He didn't want me to get out of bed tonight, but I knew you'd be here and couldn't miss it. Emmaline here made sure that I didn't."

Reynolds pushed the ailing Bruce to the stage floor. He grabbed Emmaline by the hair in an attempt to secure a hostage. She squirmed enough that Reynolds had difficulty getting his arms around her while he fumbled for his weapon. Unfortunately for him, the rigorous training his security detail had suffered through under his tutelage made them very responsive to threats. And very aggressive. A security officer to the side of the stage hit his boss with a stun gun, lurching Reynolds away from the struggling Emmaline. In quick succession, a torrent of stun guns pelted the UbiquiMed Vice President of Security and Media Relations. He lay writhing on the ground. The officers stood back, unsure they could touch him after so many volts ripping through his body. Twice an officer began to approach Reynolds, only to see him tremor violently for a few seconds. Convinced he was done flinching and the current had run its course, they scooped up their beleaguered leader, dragging him off the stage to a couple of waiting San Francisco police officers. To loud applause, Reynolds was placed in restraints, and his limp body carted away.

The group on stage waved one more time to the still-standing crowd, before exiting down the stairs to the side. As Roy went down the steps, he ran into the producer.

"Marilyn, sorry for ruining your event tonight."

"Are you kidding? That was better than any play!" She smiled appreciatively at the group. "Thank you for telling your story. It was amazing." She turned back to Roy and Bruce. "Besides, to see that bastard Reynolds go down like that was worth it."

Dale J. Moore

# *38* Home

The buzz of the alarm awoke Justin at seven sharp. He got out of bed and walked to the sonic shower. The shower started his brain. Justin walked over to his closet, staring at the items before him. It was much easier when he'd only had to grab the top item on each pile from the drawer. Picking out clothes that matched was much more difficult, and he was bad at it in the few months since his freedom.

He entered the kitchen to the smell of hot cinnamon oatmeal, with the slightest touch of honey. A tall glass of orange juice sat beside it, pulp free the way he liked it. Justin sat down at one of the four stools along the bar.

"Good morning, son." Deborah Lucas walked over to Justin, planting a kiss on the top of his head.

Kiara walked into the kitchen, still wearing her pyjamas. Justin looked at her like she was a slob.

"What? I can stay in my pj's for breakfast if I want to!"

"No fighting, you two." Peter Lucas walked over to his daughter and gave her a kiss on the top of her head. "You guys don't fight like this at work do you?"

"No. But he's my partner at Lucas Science, not my brother."

Deborah put down her bagel. "By the way, how is it, working together?"

Justin answered, "It's great. Actually just to work in the same room with someone is great. That someone being my sister is even better."

"And we don't have to call people by numbers like at UbiquiMed," Kiara said.

"I don't miss UbiquiMed one bit either," Justin added. "Reynolds deserved every bit of his sentence. I'm glad UbiquiMed's losing all of their government contracts. They won't survive long without them and their damaged reputation. It's opened up the field for new companies like ours to compete in the market."

"Well you kids had better get dressed and down to the office. Remember you have your press conference today, followed by your exclusive interview with Bruce Templeton." Deborah reminded her children of their schedule like they were in grade school.

Kiara got up from her stool, moving her plate to the cleaning centre.

"It was nice to develop the Teal and Peach cures at Lucas Science. Make sure you get Dad to the press conference on time."

Peter looked at his wife. "That reminds me, dear … do you know where my belt and dress shoes are?"

## The End

## *Review reminder*

If you enjoyed this novel, please help spread the word!

I appreciate every honest review of my work. It only takes a few seconds to provide a star rating, and a few minutes to provide a brief review. Any feedback helps incredibly for an independent author and publisher like myself!

Amazon Review Link

Thank you, Dale J. Moore

**And don't forget about the second book in the series …**

Dale J. Moore

## *Other Books by Dale J. Moore*
# *Amends*
## *A Thriller*

*If life gave you a death-defying wake-up call, would you sit back counting*
*your blessings or realize you'd been given a second chance?*

Dr. Tre Brightman seems to have it all. A young dentist with a Hollywood clientele and movie star relationships, he's living the high life. A fatal tragedy leaves him seriously injured and drives him to evaluate his actions and the casualties he's left along the side of his road to success.

He embarks on a cross-country journey of atonement, unaware that one of those victims is determined to resolve their past conflict – permanently.

Tre's quest devolves into a physical and psychological battle of endurance leaving him to wonder if he'll survive to make Amends.

# *Trials of Katrina Series*
## *Amateur Sleuth / Romantic Comedy*

Maureen P. Moore

Dale J. Moore

Dale J. Moore

Maureen P. Moore

"I enjoyed Friends of the Deceased by Dale J Moore tremendously, a novel with all the right ingredients to thrill, chill, and keep the pages turning! Witty dialogue, likable--and dislikable!--characters. Katrina keeps moving forward, and I look for more in this line of books."

**Heather Graham, New York Times and USA Today Bestselling Author**

# Life of the Party
## Book 1

### Maureen P. Moore

'Outgoing? Gorgeous? Enjoy P/T evening work? Good fun! Good pay! THIS IS PERFECTLY LEGAL!' The ad in the Toronto paper sounds just about perfect for Katrina. Except for the 'outgoing' part. Desperate to escape a creepy roommate and a scary landlord, she must find some way to supplement her meager café salary to flee to a new apartment. Eye-popping beautiful but woefully shy, when Katrina is hired as a professional guest (aka PEST) for a company called Life of the Party, her nerves get the best of her. Before she can make a total fool of herself and lose her new job, she's saved by a dashing and mysterious stranger who vanishes into the night.

With the help of her newfound friend and fellow PEST Cathy, Katrina tries desperately to find her mystery man. Her search, and her life, gets disrupted by the nefarious affairs of her roommates, landlord, and new boss. Along the way, Katrina learns that she may be shy - but she's certainly no wallflower.

# Friends of the Deceased
## Book 2
### Dale J. Moore

How does a small town girl end up investigating crime at a funeral home in Toronto? Drop-dead gorgeous Katrina is trying to run her new salon and take her relationship to a new level. The unexpected death of a client and struggles with her salon lead her to the Shady Rest funeral home.

As she stumbles her way through the personal problems that plague her world, Katrina ends up immersed in the world of preparing people for the next world.

With the help of a ruggedly handsome police detective, some old friends, and a few new ones, will she get to the bottom of what's going on, or end up buried by it? One thing is certain; when Katrina gets involved, chaos and comedy will ensue.

*"Friends of the Deceased features Katrina (Kat), a heroine who refuses to be daunted by lies and treachery and finds a silver lining because of her kindness."*
**Carolyn Hart, Author of the Death on Demand series.**

*"Behind-the-scenes hijinks at a funeral home will have you cheering for hairdresser Katrina and her gang when they delve into stolen goods, fraud, and charity scams. Katrina has to unravel the mysteries before the next ultra luxury casket is made for her."*
**Nancy J. Cohen, Author of the Bad Hair Day mystery series**

# Days of Wine and Tomatoes
## Book 3

### Dale J. Moore

Katrina is back for her third chaotic adventure! Trying to revive a struggling relationship with her detective boyfriend, they're off for a long weekend to wine country along the shores of Lake Erie. Customary to Katrina's exploits, trouble crosses her path like a black cat, altering the idyllic getaway.

As the town of Leamington holds its annual Tomato Fest, the summer waterfront party atmosphere is disrupted by a kidnapping. Mixing the enjoyment of the lake front wineries with sleuthing and rooting out clues, Katrina missteps from one mishap to another while solving mysteries in her unique way.

Having been the Life of the Party, and after surviving Friends of the Deceased, Katrina's latest escapade has barrels of wine and laughs. Mix in a bushel of tomatoes, a misfit crew, and the summer sun, and you've got Days of Wine and Tomatoes.

*"A rollicking respite perfect for a lazy spring afternoon."*
**Deborah Coonts, Author of the Lucky O'Toole Las Vegas Adventures**

# Beach Bar Blues
## Book 4

## Maureen P. Moore

Do you ever just want to get away? I mean really get away? Away from the drama and chaos that consume your life?.

Love, uncertainty, and a dash of mystical intervention collide in this humourous story of a woman on the edge of transformation. Katrina's quest for answers leads her to a quirky psychic shop that will alter her destiny forever by foretelling of a "great upheaval".

Katrina's journey is a hilarious, intimate exploration of love, expectation, and the terrifying possibility of the unexpected. She is about to discover that true love might look nothing like she expected.